King of the Trap

T.J. Edwards

**Lock Down Publications and Ca$h
Presents**
King of the Trap
A Novel by *T.J. Edwards*

T.J. Edwards

Lock Down Publications
P.O. Box 944
Stockbridge, Ga 30281

Visit our website @
www.lockdownpublications.com

Lock Down Publications
Like our page on Facebook: Lock Down
Publications @
www.facebook.com/lockdownpublications.ldp
Cover design and layout by: **Dynasty Cover Me**
Book interior design by: **Shawn Walker**
Edited by: **Lashonda Johnson**

Stay Connected with Us!

Text **LOCKDOWN** to 22828 to stay up-to-date with new releases, sneak peaks, contests and more…

Thank you.

Submission Guideline.

Submit the first three chapters of your completed manuscript to ldpsubmissions@gmail.com, subject line: Your book's title. The manuscript must be in a .doc file and sent as an attachment. Document should be in Times New Roman, double spaced and in size 12 font. Also, provide your synopsis and full contact information. If sending multiple submissions, they must each be in a separate email.

Have a story but no way to send it electronically? You can still submit to LDP/Ca$h Presents. Send in the first three chapters, written or typed, of your completed manuscript to:

LDP: Submissions Dept
P.O. Box 944
Stockbridge, Ga 30281

DO NOT send original manuscript. Must be a duplicate.

Provide your synopsis and a cover letter containing your full contact information.

Thanks for considering LDP and Ca$h Presents.

Dedications

This book is dedicated to my amazingly, beautiful stomp down wife, Mrs. Jelissa Shante Edwards, who knows firsthand what this Ski Mask life is all about.

I've had to feed our family many nights using that to make it happen. But, for you, I had to find another way because you deserve the best, and my place to be is beside you, protecting you at all times.

You're my motivating force that keeps me going. No matter how old you get, you'll always be my baby girl. So, deal with it. I love you forever and always.

Your husband.

R.I.P to my beautiful mother, Deborah L. Edwards

Shout out to Cash and Shawn. I love y'all with all my heart…not only as a C.E.O and C.O.O, but as brother and sister. This is me and my wife's home. You already know that our loyalty is sealed in blood. Mad love to the entire LDP family.

Chapter 1

Tyson

It was a dark and rainy night in April. Lightning flashed across the blinds outside of the house. The wind blew with an intensity that sent the house swaying just a bit. Though it was only April the house was so cold that I could see my breath inside of it. I took the wool blanket that was wrapped around my shoulders and pulled it firmer around me. I had been shaking for the last twenty minutes and now my teeth were chattering together.

My sister Hermés came into the living room with a blanket wrapped around her body as well. She was five-feet-four inches tall, with caramel skin, and brown eyes. She was slim and kept a jazzy attitude that more than made up for the weight that she didn't have on her.

"Man, sometimes I hate even coming to this house. Why the hell is it so cold in here when mama and daddy got all this money? It just doesn't make any sense." She flopped on the couch and grabbed the remote control off the glass table and flipped on the television. She was two years older than me, and at eighteen years old her temper already mirrored that of my mother's, whereas I was mild-mannered and patient like our father.

"What have you been sitting here doing?"

"Chilling, I wanted to hit up this party over in Brooklyn, but Pops was saying that he wanted us to be here when he got home. I don't know what he's on but I don't feel like being here right now. It's Friday and it's parties going on everywhere."

"I know, he hit my phone saying the same thing. I shoulda taken my ass to college. He and mama thought that just because I decided to take a gap year they can control everything I do. I ain't wit' that shit though, word up." She flipped through the channels until she settled on Love and Hip Hop.

"When it's time for me to go to college I'm definitely going. Ain't no way I'm staying here." While I really didn't mind our family life. I was ready to get out there and do my own thing. I was tired of answering to my parents and waiting around for them to handle everything for me. I had this urging inside of me that yearned for independence. I wanted to be a boss of some kind. I wanted to call shots and make large sums of money. I didn't know what kind of boss, or where the money was going to come from, but I knew that I would get it when it was time for me too.

Hermés set the remote on the glass table and ran her fingers through her hair. She had shoulder-length naturally curly hair that she'd inherited from our mother who was from the island of Grenada. "Yo' I feel like catching me one of those baller type niggas and break they ass. That wouldn't be nothin' for me to do. It's so much money out here in New York. I could snag an old head and hit his bank accounts. Once I clean them out, I'd bounce to California and model."

I smacked my lips and side-eyed her. "Man, you only five-feet-four inches tall, you ain't big enough to be a model."

"It's tall enough and shut up because I can be anything I wanna be. You just mad cause yo' dumb ass ain't got no dreams."

"Yo' don't be calling me dumb and shit. You know I don't like that," I snapped.

I was dyslexic and very sensitive about that. On top of that, I wasn't that great of a student. I needed extra help in school, and I was horrible at learning in a group environment. It made me feel stupid and retarded.

"N'all fuck that nigga. Word up, you're always shooting ya slugs at my height and weight. I'ma about to lay into ya ass about being dumb then." She positioned herself on the couch so that the lamp illuminated her face, and she could be seen as clear as day. "Yo' you ain't gon' be shit if you can't master that schoolwork, Tyson. Yo' dumb ass is going to be forced to stay here with mama and daddy for the rest of your life. That's gonna suck."

"Yeah, well, yo' lil' skinny ass could never lock down a baller. Nigga's wit' bags only fuckin' wit' thick hoez. So, I ain't gon' be the only mafucka that gotta stay wit' mama and daddy."

She mugged me for a long time, then pushed me hard. She stood up and balled up her fists. "Fuck you, nigga. You're always attacking my self-esteem. You can't tell me what I can and can't lock down. I know I look good, you're just a hater."

I didn't like anybody touching my face including my sister. I might've been a dumb nigga in school, but I was a good-looking dumb nigga. At five-feet-eleven inches tall I had muscles in all the right places, and was caramel-skinned, with brown eyes. I had low cut hair, with natural deep waves that if I let go too long would turn into silky curls. I had that island shit up in my blood and I was glad because it mixed well with my DNA.

Hermés stuck her finger into my face. "Yo' you're making me feel so bad that I feel like kicking yo' ass. You know how I get when I feel disrespected." She balled her fists again, breathing hard.

I stood up and looked down at her. "I don't give a fuck how you feeling. You try that shit wit' me and I'ma buss yo' black ass, word to God." I didn't like hitting my sister, but she was a scrapper.

She had a problem with taking off on me or slapping me across the face. If ever I allowed her to do this, she would try and treat me like a pussy type nigga for at least a week. So, I wasn't cool with that. Now I was on point and ready to react whenever I was sure she was close to striking.

Hermés balled her fists tighter together. "Nigga, you ain't gon' do shit to me. I'm the oldest and you already know you can't fuck wit' my bidness." She spaced her feet.

I knew she did this when she was ready to swing. My father had been teaching her how to box ever since she was five years old, just as he had me.

I tensed and got ready for her to make her move. "Hermés, if you think that oldest shit means anything to me you got me fucked—"

Crack!

She'd caught me running my mouth and punched me as hard as she could hear in my jaw. I fell back disbelieving that I had been slow to react. As I was falling into the wall, she was rushing me at full speed with her small fists swinging. Two blows landed in my face quickly. She grabbed ahold of my shirt, and gave me another to the jaw, before backhanding me. I bit my tongue and could taste my blood.

She jumped back and threw her guards up. "Fuck you wanna do."

I felt the blood drip off my lip. It wound up sliding along my neck. I gathered myself and came toward her with my guards up. Even though she was my sister I was ready to treat her ass like a stranger. "Come on, bitch."

"Bitch?" She rushed me swinging with precision.

I sidestepped her and slapped her across the face. Then picked her up around her skin midsection and fell to the floor with her. I got ready to straddle her body but when I lifted my left leg to get over her, she brought her knee upward,

12

crunching my pebbles. I hollered out like a bear shot with a tranquilizer dart.

She pushed me off her and straddled me as I laid on my side. "That's why a man can never be as strong as a woman. Because everything you mafuckas do is run by that shit between ya legs. Real bitches attack ya manhood and make you bow down." She started raining blows down on me back to back. That shit started hurting so bad that I groaned in pain. "Yeah, nigga, get yo' punk ass up!" More blows, they came so fast and hard that by the time she finished I was ready to tap out.

She stood up and looked down on me while she breathed hard. "Get up, Tyson. Fuck you still on the floor for?"

I glared at her from the side of my eyes. Then I began to get up watching her the whole time. She was lucky she was my sister, had she not have been I woulda been running into my mother's room, flipping the bed and grabbing one of the many firearms that my father had under there.

I stepped back. "Hermés, you're lucky you're my sister. I swear to God if you weren't, I would be all over yo' ass right now."

She smirked. "I ain't worried about it. You gon' quit coming at me if you can't handle what I do when I arrive. Just respect my gangsta and we'll be cool." She fixed her hair, and sat back on the couch, crossing her legs.

Before I could say what I was thinking my mother Janelle came into the front door of the house with an angry look on her face. She left the door open as she stepped into the living room. "Look I don't know what is going on but y'all father wants both of you to get in his Navigator. He's parked out front waiting. It's in your best interest to hurry up, he's not in a good mood.

Hermés and I looked at each other in worry. Whenever my mother said that my father wasn't in a good mood that could only mean the worst. I was praying that his mood wasn't because of something he'd found out that I'd done wrong. At the same time, I was also praying the best for my sister. She was always doing something, and my father never hesitated to discipline her with the same amount of vigor that he did me. Hermés had a habit of fighting back, and that often led to her getting her ass broke up to the max. I didn't know the reason he was summoning us, but I already knew that even if I did there was no way to prepare for it.

***

My father, Locust was five-feet-ten inches tall, dark-skinned, with dreadlocks that fell to the middle of his back. He had brown eyes, but poor vision, and because he did, he made it his business to wear designer framed glasses at all times. He was born and raised in Kingston, Jamaica and though he'd been back and forth to New York for over eighteen years he still spoke with a strong Jamaican accent. If you weren't accustomed to being around him it would be nearly impossible to understand what he was saying.

On the night that Hermés and I had gotten into our hundredth fight, my father came and scooped us up. He rolled in silence until we got to the Red Hook Houses where we wound up in the boiler room with twenty of his killas standing in a circle around a man that had a white hood over his head, and duct tape along his wrists and ankles. My father stepped into the circle bringing me and Hermés along with him. He stopped to look back at both of us. He smiled, then slowly his face became a mask of anger. He balled his fist and punched the bound man. The man groaned, and my father snatched the hood off his face and threw it to the ground.

Hermés covered her mouth and stood back. "Oh my God. Daddy!"

My father nodded his head. "Mi let dis yah bwoy inna fi mi inner circle tuh help fi im fambily git frackles bikaaz dem did starving lakka di rest ah dees mon yah an he tek advantage ah fi mi truss." He held out his right hand, and one of his men placed a machete into it. "Duh yuh waah tuh explain tuh mi wah dis a all bout gyal?"

Hermés shook her head. "We were just friends, Daddy. I get bored in da house all the time. I needed somebody to talk to."

My father took his phone off his waist and handed it to Hermés. "Ah mon shud nebba haffi si fi im dawta eena dis position. Dis rammy mek ah mockery ah mi an yuh afta violating fi mi truss. Bikaaz ah dat, he muss pay di consequences."

Hermés's eyes bucked as she watched the images on the phone. I could hear the sounds of her moaning and groaning. The panting was enough to make me sick to my stomach. She turned the phone off and slipped it into her front pocket. "You son of a bitch. I trusted you, Marcus. How could you do this to me?"

Slap!

My father backhanded her to the ground, knocking her dizzy. I rushed to her side and helped her to her feet. She leaned on me with weak knees and groaned.

"Mi will nah akcep ah whore fi ah dawta. Mi wud radda kill yuh. Yuh mek mi luk lakka an claffy eena front ah dis peasant." He turned to Marcus and held the machete against his cheek. He slowly slid it across his skin until it tore and bled. "Yuh nuh mess wid di negus bwoy. Wen yuh duh yuh git di plague." He leaned into his face. Marcus was whimpering into his duct tape, blood oozed out of his nostrils. "Hermés, bring unnu ass yah an cleanse yuhself ah yuh sins."

Hermés mugged him. "What?"

"Now!" My father hollered.

Slowly Hermés stepped away from me. She walked up to my father with the entire basement watching her. "Yes, Daddy?"

My father took a step back and handed her the machete. He pointed to Marcus's jugular. "Yuh will kunk him yah an yah."

"But Daddy, I—" Hermés began.

My father pulled out a .45 pistol and placed it to the back of her head. "Eff yuh did eena jamrock yuh wud areddi bi dead. Now duh wah di fuck mi seh ar else." He cocked the hammer. "Now!"

Hermés tightened up her grip on the machete. She stepped up next to Marcus timid. "I'm sorry, Marcus, but you did this." She placed the blade to his jugular and dug in before she pulled back swiftly, blood skeeted.

"Tap rampin an kill him, now!" My father roared.

"Okay!" Hermés cocked back her arm and swung the machete as fast and hard as she could crashing it into his neck and slicing partway through it. The machete got stuck. She struggled to pull it out. Marcus shook wildly hollering into his duct tape.

Hermés backed up, holding her ears. She bumped into me. I wrapped my arms around her. We all stood back and watched Marcus go nuts until his body gave up the fight. By this time blood was all over the boiler room.

My father stood over him. He yanked the machete out of his throat. "Dis a ah small example ah wah ih luk lakka tuh cross di negus. Yuh nuh waah tuh bi him. Mi can bank pan dat." He laughed, and spit in Marcus's face. "Clean dis bubu up. He disgusts mi." He eyed Hermés. "Dis a yuh fos kuff. Nuh let ih hap'm again."

Hermés started to shake. "I gotta get out of here." She broke away from me and ran out of the basement.

I took off behind her, my father didn't chase us. He was sure that he had made his point.

Chapter 2

When I turned seventeen years old my mother bought me my first car. It was a 2017 Camaro, black-on-black with the all-white leather seats. My pops was furious at her because I was fucking up in school, and my grades were terrible. Second, to that, I hadn't jumped off the stoop to start fucking around inside his Fast Money Cartel. I was too busy trying to grow up. I still had a lot of immature ways about myself, and I didn't think I was ready to start cutting off heads and going to war with different cartels, and drug empires.

It was two thousand and seventeen and Heroin and all forms of opiates were taking the city of New York by storm. Everybody I knew was doing some kind of pill or fucking with that smack. So, while my father was immersed in one bloody war after the next, I was just this teenage lil' nigga trying to get my mind right.

On the third day of having my whip, one of our neighbors named Jazzy was coming from the grocery store with a bunch of bags in her hand when she stopped in front of the Camaro and looked me up and down as I stepped out of it. Jazzy was five-feet-two inches tall and strapped. She was originally from Baton Rouge, Louisiana, so she had that nice southern weight on her. She was brown-skinned, with shoulder-length hair, and she was slightly bow-legged. Damn near every nigga in Brooklyn had their eyes on her, and it still amazed me that none of them had enough common sense to do what I did on this bright and sunny day.

I rushed around the car and began to take her bags from her hands before she could tell me not to. I knew her apartment was on the third floor, and for a woman trying to carry them all the way up there, it would have proved to be difficult. Hell, it was going to be difficult for me.

"Let me get these bags from you, Jazzy. I wish you woulda told me that you were going to the store and that you didn't have a ride. I woulda took you asap." I made sure I had a good grasp on the bags.

She shielded her eyes from the sun as she looked up at me. "Boy, this car has been sitting out here for three days. I didn't know it was yours. When did you get it?" She looked it over with lust in her eyes.

"I copped it a few days ago. I had to save my ends to get it. You like it?" I looked over at it.

She nodded. "Yeah, it fits you." She was quiet for a second, a gust of wind blew her hair all over her pretty face. "I can already tell you're going to have a bunch of lil' girls in it, ain't you?" She gave me the side-eye.

I shrugged my shoulders. "I don't know, right now I'm trying to focus on finishing school so I can go to college. Brooklyn needs to be put in my rearview mirror quickly." I started to walk up the steps.

She followed. "Yeah, I hear that. How old are you now?"

Her stoop had a bunch of females on it that were whispering to each other. Most of the dope and jack boys were out and they were eyeing Jazzy from afar. She was wearing a pair of denim jeans that made her ass look perfect. She was super thick, so thick that it was intimidating.

I wanted to lie about my age. I didn't want her to know that I was still a kid. I was sure that would make her dismiss me if I had had a chance with her. But I kept shit real. "I'm seventeen, I'll be eighteen in a few months." It would be more than a few but who was counting.

"Aw, that's what's up." She opened the main door and her daughter Tasia came out of it.

Tasia was seventeen just like me. She was a spitting image of her mother only slimmer. Her breasts were small, and a lot of people at school picked on her about them. Personally, I thought she was perfect. I found beauty in every female. It was the dudes that I didn't like.

Tasia looked me up and down. "Mama, why is he carrying our groceries?" She mugged me and crossed her arms in front of her flat chest.

"Because it appears that he is the only gentleman in this neighborhood, that's why. Do you wanna help me?" Jazzy asked.

Tasia rolled her eyes. "N'all, I'm Gucci. I'm finna go to the park and chill. Y'all will be alright." She brushed past me and headed down the steps. "Come on y'all."

Her group of female friends that had been sitting on the stoop whispering to each other got up and followed behind her. Tasia was at the bottom of the stoop when she looked back up at me while her friend whispered into her ear.

She sucked her teeth. "Girl, ugh, he is not all that." She rolled her eyes and they headed down the block.

Though my eyes were on her ass my self-esteem had been attacked. I was trying to figure out what about me was so hideous that it would make her utter the words ugh?

Jazzy sighed. "Come on up, baby. Don't worry about them."

***

I watched Jazzy put the groceries away item by item. I couldn't take my eyes off her ass no matter how hard I tried. There was something about this older woman that was driving me crazy. I was so hard from watching her I couldn't take my hand off my lap. I didn't have any problem masturbating and handling my business on my own, everything aroused me.

Jazzy took two five-pound bags of sugar and got stuck trying to put them in a cupboard. She had managed to get the bags partway in but was now in a crucial space where she needed to get them in so that they wouldn't fall out. They were right on the edge. Her ass looked perfect from where I was sitting.

"Tyson, help me before I drop this stuff on my head."

I jumped up and headed over to her. She was straining to reach. I got behind her, boner and all, and pushed the bags into the cupboard. Once they were in, I even surprised myself because I stayed behind her. The feel of my hard piece trapped in the crack of her ass felt so good to me, I closed my eyes. I would have to remember that when I did my thing at night. I pushed forward a little bit to help her better.

She moaned and placed her hands on the counter. Her back arched, she trembled and turned around to face me. Her eyes bore into mine. "My husband has been locked up for four years now. I have been holding him down as best I can. He got a year left."

I nodded. "Why are you telling me that?" I could smell her perfume being up this close, she smelled good. My piece got harder.

She walked up on me and gripped my thing through my pants. I groaned, it felt good. "Because I could feel this lil' hard thang all on my ass and I ain't felt nothing like that in a long time. You got all kinds of crazy thoughts running through my mind right now. I feel so dirty." She never took her grip off my pipe.

"I apologize, Ms. Jazzy, but you're just so fine. Every time I watch you it drives me crazy." My piece throbbed, and I felt like buckling. The scent of her perfume was stronger now that she had me feeling a way.

She still had a hold of it. "I really don't see you hanging around with too many lil' boys other than that Maze. Are you the type to run yo' mouth, or are you mature enough to keep what happens with you to yourself?" She released my dick and ran her hand up my stomach. She stepped forward, and I felt slightly intimidated.

"I-I-I don't like that gossiping mess. I know how to keep a secret," I stuttered.

Jazzy smiled and kissed my neck. "I can see myself turning yo' lil' ass out, but I guess time will tell. You're so handsome. Even when you were just a boy I always knew you were going to be handsome." She kissed my neck again and slid her hand back down my stomach. She started to unbutton my pants.

I felt breathless. I started remembering all the times that I'd seen her walk through our block in Brooklyn and how all of the dope boys and trap stars would be whistling and saying what they'd do to her pussy. I grew worried, she was a grown woman with a daughter my age. I knew damn well there was no way I could measure up to what she was looking for.

She had the flaps of my jeans open, she pulled them down and saw the hard lump in my boxers. "I just wanna see how it looks. It's been a while since I saw one in the flesh. You got me thirsty to see you down there."

I started trembling. "It's cool." I was praying that my dick was big enough.

She pulled it out, and I watched her eyes light up. She smiled and started sucking on her bottom lip. "Damn lil' daddy, I don't know what they are putting in the water but kudos to you. She crouched down and pumped me. She brought it close to her face and sniffed the head, then she shivered, and so did I. "You ever been with a girl before?" She raised her right eyebrow.

At first, I thought about lying to her because I hadn't. I didn't want her to hold that against me and allow that to make her treat me like a baby. I was ready for whatever she had in mind. Before I could come up with a lie, she decided to answer the question for me.

"N'all, you haven't, and that's okay. I think it's cute." She pulled the skin back and kissed the head. Her tongue swiped at it before she sucked just the tip into her mouth.

My knees buckled, I reached out and took a hold of her shoulders. "Damn, Jazzy."

She snickered. "What? I ain't doing nothing but checking you out. Ooohhh, it's been so long." She opened her pants and slid her hand in between her thighs. She moaned and closed her eyes. "Just let me see this for a minute, baby." She rubbed the head against her cheek, then she sucked me into her mouth again. She sucked me slow and steady. The feeling kept getting better and better.

I was doing all I could to not cum fast. I'd always heard from the whisperings of the girls at school that cumming too fast was embarrassing but I was to the point where it was becoming impossible to avoid. "Jazzy, I'm trying my best." I trembled.

She was sucking me fast and loudly at this point. Her fingers were working overtime inside her pants and I was praying that I could see what she was doing. "It's okay, baby. It's okay," she said these words around my pole and went right back to sucking at full speed. She was slurping and moaning, and it became too much.

I came. "Mmm."

Her sucking stopped, she plopped me out and pumped me. More cum shot out of the tip and fizzed over the head of the stalk. She waited for as much to come as she could before she licked it up and sucked me dry.

I fell to my knees, and then my back. She kept attacking me. When she was sure that no more of my seed would come out, she backed up to her haunches. "Damn, I'm so wrong." She pulled her fingers out of her. I saw that they were greasy from her juices.

"You're not wrong. I wanted to do that, too." My throat was dry, suddenly I was shy as hell. I could smell the scent of her arousal.

She held her fingers over to my lips. "Taste this Tyson. You're talking about how fine I am, and how I drive you crazy, right? Well, you can't begin to understand anything about me until you can grow crazy from my true scent and taste. So, here."

I opened my mouth before her fingers even went inside of my orifice, I could smell her. My dick got harder. I sucked on her fingers. The taste was salty and pungent. I liked it, I started licking her fingers clean.

This must have turned her on because she started pumping my piece again. "Boy, you gon' make me give you some pussy, ain't you? I'm trying so hard to be faithful, but you're just somethin' else." She wiggled out of her jeans with her free hand leaving my dick jumping, then she sucked me back into her mouth. When I was as hard as I possibly could be, she laid back and pulled her panties down. "I want you to taste me." She opened her thick thighs wide and trailed her finger through her folds.

I was on my knees, and between those thighs as if there was a magnet drawing my face into the apex of her sex. "I need you to tell me what to do. I ain't never did this before," I whispered ready to be taught.

She licked her lips and purred. "Damn, boy, you keep sending shivers through me. "Okay, look, dis is what we are going to do." She leaned back on her elbows and opened herself wider. "You see this little nipple at the top of my lips, this is the most important sexual part of a woman's body. Whenever you are looking to give her any sort of pleasure this is the nub that you need to focus on." She rolled her middle finger around it and trembled. "Do you understand that?"

I nodded. "Yeah." I leaned my face as close to her nub as I could taking in her scent when somebody started knocking on the front door.

Jazzy scooted backward and jumped up getting herself together. "Who is it?"

"It's me, mama. I forgot my key," Tasia sounded irritated. "Open up I gotta pee real bad."

Minutes later I was the one that opened the door, and as soon as it was open, she ran into the house and passed me, and I hurried right out of there with a slight smile on my face. I could still smell Jazzy's scent on my top lip and it was driving me crazy. So much so that I went home and did my thing while thinking about her.

Chapter 3

Even though Hermés was a real short-tempered and stuck up female to damn near everybody outside of our home, there were times when she was just an emotional female that was thirsty for reassurances. Three days after that first sexual experience took place with Ms. Jazzy, Hermés came into my bedroom with her hair all over her head and bags under her eyes. I was sleeping like a baby when she flipped on the bedroom light and opened the door so hard that the doorknob crashed into the wall and crumbs of drywall fell to the floor. This made me sit up straight in the bed.

"I'm tired of this house, Tyson. I need to get the fuck out of this house, and New York period." She stood there looking at me in her nightgown as if I knew what was going on with her.

I squinted my eyes to see what time it was. The sight of 3:30 in the morning had me ready to curse my sister out. I was groggy and had only gotten to sleep a few hours prior. I'd been up all night doing the most with myself and thinking about Jazzy. I still couldn't believe that all that had taken place. "Yo' what's the matter with you, Shorty?"

"Don't call me that shorty shit. You know I don't like it when you do." She sighed, came over, and sat on the edge of the bed. She turned to look at me. "I feel suicidal, Tyson. Look at this." She held out her right wrist and I saw the deep cut that slowly began to bleed out. The cut wasn't enough to assume that she was getting ready to die at any minute but enough to cause concern.

I grabbed it and mugged the hell out of her. "What the hell is wrong with you? Are you crazy?"

She shrugged her shoulders. "I swear to God I feel like it. I'm so sick of living right now. I'm tired of being in this house.

I am tired of being controlled. I need to get my shit together, so I don't ever have to worry about this pain that I am feeling deep inside of me. I feel so ugly and so low."

I got up, left the room, and came back with a washcloth, peroxide, and a band-aid. I took a seat beside her and cleaned up her injury, then bandaged it up. As soon as I was done, I climbed into the bed and pulled her into my embrace. I kissed her cheek. "Yo' Hermés, yousa Goddess, ma. I think you are one of the most beautiful and strongest females that I have ever known. I don't know what you're going through right now, but I know you are strong enough to fight through it, especially 'cause I got your back." I rested my lips on her cheek.

She snuggled closer to me. "You ever get tired of living, Tyson? Have you ever just felt like you no longer wanted to be in existence because the day by day was just too much?"

I sat up just a bit. "N'all, I haven't. Why is that how you've been feeling?"

"Yeah." She shook her head. "I started feeling like this when I was only eight years old. I have always hated myself and this lil' skinny body I am trapped inside of. As the years progressed my reasoning for being alive seemed to dwindle more and more. I'm to the point where I am straight trying to build up the nerve to get it over with."

I eased my embrace. "Why are you saying shit like this?"

She shrugged her shoulders and two tears dropped from her eyes. "Because it's how I feel. You don't understand the level of pain that I am going through. I am struggling with security within myself. I am struggling with body issues, and I don't feel like I've ever been truly loved. What is my purpose for being here?"

I climbed out of the bed, scratched my chest, and then my head through the do-rag that was keeping my waves hitting like domestic violence. "Yo' Hermés you blowing me, right now. I can't believe these words are coming out of your mouth."

She wiped her tears away from her cheeks. "I can't help the way I feel, Tyson. I can already barely explain it. I wish you were inside my body right now, because only then would you understand what I am getting at. I don't need you judging me. I just need you to understand, that's it."

I stood there watching her for a moment, then climbed into the bed. "Come here, sis."

She turned around, and slowly got back in front of me laying on her side. She backed all the way up until I was able to wrap my arms around her protectively. "You are beautiful. You are amazing, and I would kill a mafucka over you in a heart heat. You want a reason to live; how about staying alive because I need you? I need you, and I love you with all my heart and soul. I am strong because of you. You are precious to me."

"Why, though? Me and you fight all the time. I'm always trying to pick on you, and I don't cut you no breaks. How can you say that you need me when I've been nothing but trouble for you?"

"Because you are my sister, and I love you. You are precious. After we get done fighting, I always love you more. Yo' if you leave this earth, I would be lost without you. Word to Jehovah. Man, I look up to ya ass even though I'm taller than you." I kissed her scalp. "I need you, sis. I always have and I always will."

She smiled. "Thank you for saying that Tyson." She yawned. "Now hold me until it's time for you to go to school. I need to be trapped right now, I don't trust myself." She placed her hand on top of mine and got comfortable on her pillow. Her eyes closed, and within minutes we were both sleeping soundly.

***

The next day at school I was tired as hell and yawning through all my classes. When the school day was over, I was digging in my locker to make sure I had the right books for my homework that night when Tasia walked up to me with her books in front of her chest. Her arms were wrapped around them. At first, she stood staring at me without saying any words. Classes were over so the hallways were packed with students rushing to get to their cars, or on to the school buses.

"What's good? Why are you just staring at me like I'm some kind of traffic accident?"

She kept chewing her gum for a moment longer, and then she stopped. "Which one of these girls around here are you talking to?" She was already wearing her blue and white cheerleading outfit that had her looking all kinds of sexy to me.

"What?" I was caught off guard.

I looked past her shoulder and her clique of females was a short distance away by the bathrooms rocking their cheerleading uniforms watching us. I didn't know what she was up to but I was sure that her clique did.

"The reason I'm asking is because you come fitted every single day. You rocking Gucci, Prada, Chanel, and Balenciagas and shit. I already know one of these females had to stake their claim on you. So, which one did it?"

I eyed her, then her buddies from afar. I closed my locker and scoffed. "Yo', I definitely don't fuck wit lil' ass girls. One of yo' buddies wanna holler at me then tell them to approach me like a lady. That middle school, shy shit is played out." I walked away from her.

She stood there for a moment. When I looked back at her she had her hands on her hips in disbelief. "No, he didn't." She jogged to catch up with me. "Don't be walking away from me like you're all that." She grabbed my wrist.

I stopped and looked down at her. "Man, what do you want? Why the fuck are you bothering me?"

She winced and looked over her shoulder at her crew again. Then she bit into the skin on her bottom lip nervously. "Look the only reason I was asking that question is because my homegirl, Charity, wanted to ask you to the prom. You know they're doing this whole gender reversal thing this year where the females are asking the males? But if you're saying that you don't like that junior high, shy stuff then I'm just gon' come on out and get at you." She took a deep breath and looked up at me. "Tyson, will you go to the prom with me?"

Now I was really caught off guard. Tasia was the head cheerleader and hands down one of the baddest females in school. All the jocks were trying their best to get her attention by flossing as much as they could in front of her and I was sure she was going.

To hear her asking me to the prom made me feel like a boss. "Yeah, that sounds cool. But you gotta tell ya girl Charity over there that you snaked her." I laughed.

She shrugged her shoulders. "And, is that all?"

I smiled. "What you finna do, right now?"

She popped back on her legs. "We got cheerleading practice until six, but I'm free after that. Why, you trying to chill?"

As she was saying this Lil' Chris came down the hallway with a few of his Flatbush niggas. Lil' Chris was five-feet-seven, with a stocky build. He had short dreads and was known for being a shooter all over Brooklyn. His brother was part of the Jack Boy Mafia but had been indicted by the Feds and given life in prison without the possibility of release. Lil' Chris was riding high off his brother's name. He came and slid his arm around Tasia's shoulders and kissed her on the cheek.

"What's the deal, Goddess? Why you standing here talking to this nigga for so long?"

Tasia rolled her eyes and tried to get his arm from around her neck. He refused. She let it stay put. "Look I ain't with all of this public display of affection shit. Get off me." She removed his arm and fixed her hair.

Lil' Chris frowned. "Answer my mafuckin' question?"

Tasia smirked. "Boy quit it, I got cheerleading practice. Tyson, I'll get up with you later." She started to walk away.

Lil' Chris grabbed her aggressively and slammed her up against the locker. He kissed her lips passionately and slipped his hand up her skirt until he had her panting and breathing hard. When he broke his kiss, her nipples were spiked up against her blouse. She pushed him off her and walked away on weak knees.

Lil' Chris stepped into my face. "Yo', you sniffing around my dame, kid?"

I didn't like him, or too many other niggas for that matter. When he got into my face I got vexed right away. "Say, Dunn, how 'bout you give me some space? I don't know you like that."

Lil' Chris flared his nostrils. He slipped his hand under his shirt. "I'm the Flatbush, Prince. You know who you fuckin' wit', right now?"

"Nah, Son, and I don't care either. Get the fuck up out of my face talking 'bout this chick. I'm just minding my own bidness." I was getting angrier and angrier.

"I got tools that'll knock ya bidness all over these hallways, Kid. Word to the borough? I catch you sniffing around Tasia again and I'ma bust ya ass. Now try me."

"Nigga fuck you." I pushed him out of my face.

He stumbled back and got ready to rush me along with four of his homies. Suddenly they stopped, Lil' Chris's eyes got as big as saucers. He backed up and pointed at me. "Tyson right, yeah, a'ight." He nodded his head and walked off.

I watched him and his crew until they left the hallway. When I turned around Maze, and two of his Red Hook killas were standing a few feet away from me in black Chanel leather jackets. He walked up to me and gave me a half hug.

"Yo', I don't know what that was all about but you gotta watch ya back now. That nigga Lil' Chris is as shiesty as they come. You need a burner?"

Lil' Chris and I had known each other ever since the first grade. He was the only nigga I jammed wit'. I disliked men as a gender, period. He was dark as sin, slim with long dreads, and a big beard that he grew in honor of his father that was a Muslim. His father was locked up for life.

"N'all, son, I'm good. I ain't sweating that chump. What's the deal, though?"

"I got some shit I wanna holler at you about. I gotta take care of some other shit first. I'll hit you up later. Fuck wit' me when I hit ya phone. Gimme ya word, though."

"You got that." I eyed Tasia as she went into the gymnasium to begin her cheerleading practice, she winked at me.

"Yo', word to God, that lil' bitch is trouble. That nigga Lil' Chris will kill ya ass over her."

"Yeah, well Shorty sweating me. I can't help if a bitch jocking a nigga. That's something that he gotta deal with."

Maze scratched his beard. "You sho' you don't need that burner, though?"

"Yeah, I'm good."

"A'ight den." He gave me a half hug again. "Remember to pick up when I call you. I got some fat to put on your mental. It's important to be there, Dunn, word up."

"I will." He broke our embrace and bounced with his guys following behind him. On the way out of the school, I took a second to peek into the gym, Tasia was in there instructing her crew on how to hit the splits. She did it effortlessly, looked up, and caught me peeping her ass. I let the door close and bounced.

Chapter 4

Jazzy pulled me into her apartment and pushed me up against the wall. She locked the door and sucked on my neck. "Damn, lil' Daddy, I've been thinking about you ever since you left here a week ago. I have been battling with my morals and all that stuff." She bit into my neck and sucked harder while her hand slipped into my boxers. She gripped my dick. "Tell me that you're still a virgin. Don't lie to me either." She unzipped me and pumped my piece causing it to grow longer and longer.

I groaned, "I still am."

She leaned over. "Good." She sucked me into her mouth while she unzipped her short shorts and allowed them to fall to her ankles. She kicked them by her glass table and stood before me naked. There was a nice bit of hair growing over her sex lips. It looked different but sexy to me. This was a grown woman. That gave me chills.

"I'm about to give you some of this pussy, Tyson. I don't know if you're ready for it, but we finna see. We gotta hurry up too cause Tasia will be back from cheerleading practice in an hour or so." She grabbed my hand and pulled me down the hall to her bedroom.

Once there she pushed me back on the bed and flipped on some old school *Mary J. Blige*. She crawled next to me and took a hold of my dick. "Damn, you got all of this. I wouldn't know what to do if I had yo' lil' young butt walking around my house with all of this dick every day." She pumped it five times and sucked me into her mouth opening her thighs wide.

I groaned and slipped my hand between her legs. I rubbed her hot pussy. She was oozing wet, her lips were meaty. The hair was a bit scratchy, but magnetic nonetheless. I couldn't wait until I was able to slide inside her. I placed two fingers into her box.

"Uhhhhh—shit." She'd popped me out of her mouth to emit this moan. She rolled onto her back and held her knees in the air opening her thighs. "Taste me, baby. I need you, too."

I crawled until my face was between her thighs. I snuck my head into her middle and kissed the lips. They were spongy. Her scent was strong and intoxicating. I separated the lips and found her clitoris quickly. It popped out of her hood like a small pinky finger, I flicked it.

"Mmm, there you go." She opened her thighs wider.

I licked all around it, sucked it into my mouth, and acted like it was going to give me some milk. I suckled, swallowing her juices during the process. The salty flavor made me harder than a steel pole.

"Yes! Yes! Uhhh, lil' Daddy! Fuck!" She threw her head back. "I'm cumming! Shit, it's been so long." She began to shiver.

I kept flicking and sucking until she smashed my face into her gap. She began to ride it. I couldn't breathe, but at the same time, I was willing to allow her to suffocate me as long as that meant that I was doing it right.

"Uhhh, baby! Ohhh, baby! This shit feels so good." She threw back her head and screamed, before cumming again in strong jerks. Then she pushed me off her.

I stood on my knees beating my pipe looking between her thick legs. I had never seen a grown woman's pussy ooze like hers was. Though I was standing two feet away from her I swear it felt like I could feel the heat from between her thighs as if it were an oven. I wanted to cum so bad watching her.

Jazzy sat up and threw me to the bed. "Now I'm finna ride yo lil' ass. Once I put this grown pussy on you I'ma lock yo' ass down. Every vet should have her a boy toy laying in the weeds. Men do it, why can't we?" She straddled me.

Her thick thighs stuck against my ribcage. She reached behind her and took a hold of my dick. She gripped it, and slowly positioned the head so that it was right over her opening. She slid down on me inch by inch. The further down she slid the more her mouth came open until she was sitting on my sack.

"Damn, damn, damn. Okay, okay, shit, this a lot. Let me get used to it." She sat still.

I felt like I was in the tightest, hottest, wettest fist in the world. It felt soft, yet firm. My eyes kept rolling into the back of my head as if I were a slot machine. I shuddered and whimpered a moan, "Ms. Jazzy, it's too good." I dug my nails into the soft cushions of her thighs.

She placed her hands on my chest and leaned forward easing her hot pussy up my dick. She licked the sweat from my neck. "This that vet pussy, lil' Daddy. This is what a woman feels like." She arched her back and began to ride me slowly while Mary J Blige crooned through the speakers in her bedroom. "Uh—uh—uh, shit, baby. Ooo-ooo-ooo." Her hips rode me faster and faster.

My mouth was opened wide, slob slid down the side of my face, and I didn't even care. Ms. Jazzy had my lil' young ass laid out. I rubbed around until I was gripping that ghetto booty. Just the feel of it was too much. I shook and came in strong spurts deep inside of her.

"Aw! Aw! Aw! I feel you." She leaned down and bit into my neck hard, sucking it.

She came again and worked her hips slowly milking me. She kissed my lips, and the next thing I knew she was tonguing me down while she rode me slowly. During every bounce I found myself falling more and more in lust with her.

When she finally rolled off me, she sucked her juices off me and crawled out of the bed. "Come on, we're about to take a shower. I can't have you going home smelling like me."

I didn't care about that, but I didn't turn her down either. I couldn't wait to shower with a grown-ass woman.

***

When I got home that night, Hermés was already in my bedroom. The lights were off. I turned them on, and she held up a hand as if to shield her eyes from the bright glares of the sun.

"Please, turn it off, it's killing me," she slurred.

I hit the switch and eased over to her taking my shirt off. I clicked on the lamp and sat beside her. "What's the matter with you? Why are you slurring and shit?"

"Percocets, I did two sixties. I'm fucked up, right now, and I'm numb. I have been waiting on yo' ass for two hours. Where were you?"

I thought about bragging to her about what Ms. Jazzy and I had just done but I decided against it. Nothin' positive could come from that. "I was just out. Why were you looking for me?"

She shrugged her shoulders. "I need some love. I felt like being held. My depression is fucking with me real tough." She climbed on me and wrapped her arms around my neck. "I feel so low."

I was completely taken off guard. My arms were at my side at first. Slowly I closed them around her. "What's the matter?"

"Ever since Daddy forced me to do that to Marcus. I keep seeing his face whenever I close my eyes. I don't wanna see him no more. I thought I loved him, Tyson." She rested her cheek against mine.

I rubbed her back. "I'm sorry sis." Those were the only words that I could think of because I had never held Hermés the way that I was.

I felt like the position she was in shoulda been reserved for my woman, not my sister. I felt so awkward.

She slid her face against mine until she was looking into my eyes. "Can you make me feel good again, Tyson? Tell me how much I mean to you, please?" She held onto my shoulders.

I held her around the waist. "Yo', I love you, Hermés. I think you are amazing, strong, and flawlessly beautiful. Goddess, I know you are going to do great things because that's what's inside you. You are perfect, and I'd do anything for you."

She sighed and held the sides of my face. She placed her forehead against mine. "Thank you for saying that." She kissed me and rested her face in the crux of my neck. "Do you remember that song by R. Kelly that you sang in the talent show when you were twelve years old?"

"Yeah, it's called Dedicated. Why?"

"Can you sing it to me? But do it for me like you did for mama?" She sat up and looked into my eyes again.

"I got you." I licked my lips.

"Go ahead then." She looked on anticipated.

"You have given me the best of youuuu. And you have made my dreams come true. And after all, the things that you have done. Girl, it makes me say that you are more than a woman, so I—"

She kissed me again and then began singing the song in the crux of my neck. "I love you so much, Tyson. I'm sorry that I am so mean to you all the time. I swear you are my heart.

You're the only person in this world that makes me feel loved. If you weren't my brother I swear I would marry you." She hugged me tighter. "Now hold me until I fall asleep.

***

That night Maze picked me up at three in the morning. I crept out of the house in just my Tommy Hilfiger pajamas. It was raining like crazy outside. His Cadillac smelled like Kush. When I got inside, he pulled away from the curb.

I was still wiping the rain out of my face. "Kid, what's so mafuckin' important that you gotta pull me out of the bed for?"

"I gotta bust this move and I don't trust no nigga to watch my back but you. It gotta be tonight, and I ain't trying to hear nothin' you gotta say if it ain't, Kid I got you. Word to Brooklyn."

I looked over at him like he had lost his fuckin' mind. "Yo', you ain't gon' tell a nigga what this move entails?"

"I made a play for a brick. This nigga also wanna buy a few Burners. We are meeting in Coney Island. When we get a few blocks from Coney, I'ma need you to be on point. Nine times out of ten I'm about to flatline his bitch ass."

"*Flatline?* You mean kill him?"

"Yeah, nigga, what else?" Maze looked over at me like I was the one with the issues.

"Kid, we got school tomorrow. It's three in the fuckin' morning, and this is what you're doing?"

"I'm hungrier than a mafucka who ain't ate for three days. The streets are cold, and I gotta feed my daughter. The game is pistol play. You fuckin' wit' me or not?"

We rolled in silence for a moment. My whole life flashed before my eyes. I was having a hard time imagining anything positive coming from this move. The whole scene with Hermés still had my head fucked up. She'd acted like she wanted to kill me when I slipped from behind her to come and meet up with Maze. I knew Maze was crazy. If I'd turned him down there would be bad blood between us for weeks. This was my nigga. I didn't want that. "Yeah, Kid, I'm fuckin' wit' you."

"Good." He stepped on the gas and headed to our destination.

***

When we got to the destination the rain had eased up. Maze jumped out of the car and winked at me. A light-skinned dude was sitting on the hood of a Chrysler 300 that was heavily tinted. He had a duffel bag in his hand. Maze walked up to him, and they began to talk, and converse.

I checked my surroundings, we were in a big parking lot. A block away was the highway. Three blocks from there were a bunch of project buildings. I looked back over to Maze. He was nodding his head. He pointed into the bag, when the light-skinned man looked inside of it Maze upped his .9 millimeter and dumped him three times in the face. The gunfire lit up the parking lot over and over and over. The light-skinned man fell to the pavement. Maze popped him again. The back door to the Chrysler opened, and two dudes jumped out and took off running.

Maze took off behind them firing his gun back to back. One of them fell, he kept firing at the other, but the man was running in a zig-zag. Finally, he was out of bullets. He stopped over the one he'd shot and fell to his knees beside the man. The victim was kicking his legs struggling to get up. Maze began to choke him out. He growled and choked him out for two minutes. He stood up and stomped him multiple times, before checking his pockets, snatching up the Duffle bag, and jumping in the car smashing away from the scene.

"Shit, shit, shit! I didn't even know nobody was in dat mafucka. Fuck!" The wheels squeaked as he turned out of the parking lot.

I was scared that we were about to get caught. I kept seeing the dudes falling in my mind's eye. I saw the blood, I knew they were dead, and I was a part of it all.

I was in shock. "Now what?"

His eyes were searching as he drove. "Where is this nigga? He couldn't have gone far." He made a few circles around the block before he jumped on the highway in defeat. "Fuck!" He slammed his fist on the steering wheel. "Dats a'ight. I just hit they ass for two bricks of Heroin, and some cash. Half is yours if you want it."

"Dawg you just slumped two niggas. Fuck that other shit, right now? What are we going to do about the other dude?" I didn't know if he had seen my face or not, but I didn't wanna take no chances.

"Don't worry, it ain't gon' take me but a few days to track him down, when I see his face I'll know that it's him. Kid, ain't gon' get away you ain't even gotta worry about that." Maze looked over at me and smiled. "I love that killing shit, it makes me feel so alive." He laughed and grabbed a blunt from the ashtray. "Whenever you are ready for your cut, it's yours." He turned up the music and nodded his head to it while he rolled through Brooklyn with two more souls under his belt.

I felt a bit lost, I had never killed anybody before, and the fact that my right-hand man could do it so easily was still baffling to me. I sat back in my seat and scanned the streets with a million thoughts going through my mind. By the time he pulled up to my parent's place, I was ready to break away from him. I told him to hold my spoils, and I would get them when I was ready for them. He agreed.

Chapter 5

Ms. Jazzy's husband came home nine months later. His entire first month home she didn't hit me up or say nothin' to me when I saw her on the block of our neighborhood with him. She averted her eyes and kept it moving. I felt a way, but I didn't dwell too much on it. In my opinion, she was the baddest bitch in our entire hood and I had been blessed with the pleasures of fucking her. I felt like a true God, couldn't anybody tell me shit.

Three weeks after Tasia's father came home I was pulling into Burger King parking lot ready to pick me and Hermés up something to eat when Tasia ran out of the restaurant with tears in her eyes, and her clothes ripped. She crashed into the hood of my Camaro and was about to jump over it. Three females ran out of the Burger King hot on her heels. Tasia ran until she got just outside of the parking lot, then she threw up her dukes. When the first female ran up, she punched her twice and jumped back ready for the next. The second girl rushed her with her head down. Tasia jumped into the air and kneed her busting her nose wide open.

"Come on, Bitch! You can get some of this, too!" She screamed at the last girl who looked like a grown-ass woman.

She had Tasia by at least fifty pounds. The big girl threw up her dukes and rushed Tasia like a trained fighter. Tasia hit her three times. The big girl took those hits, then punched Tasia dropping her to the ground and began stomping her. Cars were honking their horns and people were gathered around watching the fight. Nobody was looking to pull this adult-sized female off Tasia.

I threw my car in park and made haste across the lot. When I got to the big girl that was acting like she was ready to stomp

Tasia into the ground I pushed her big ass off her so hard that she flew back and landed in the street.

"Get yo big ass up off her. Fuck wrong wit' you?"

The big girl bounced up and dusted off her clothes. "That's a'ight nigga. I'ma have my brother blow yo' head off. You better watch yo' back. This Flatbush all day!" She backed up and rushed to her car.

Her friends followed her to the red Pontiac Grand Prix where the big girl started the car and stormed away from the lot.

I mugged them until they were out of sight, then I picked Tasia up. She was just coming out of her slumber. "Come on, Goddess, get yo ass up.

She was dizzy in my arms. She didn't wake up fully until she was sitting in the passenger's seat of my Camaro. "What happened? Where dem bitches at? They don't want no more of this." She winced in pain when she touched her busted lip. "Ooowwww."

"Shorty, you, betta quit talking all of that tough shit. Ole girl just knocked you out. I just chased her away because she was kicking yo' ass."

"Damn, you blunt. Can you have some compassion? You act like you ain't never lost a fight before." She continued to touch her swollen lip.

"N'all, I have, but not one as bad as she was doing you. Word is bond, had I not ran over there you were about to be flat as a pancake."

She smacked her lips. "Now, you just doing too much." She pulled down the sun visor and the little mirror light came on. She checked her mug. "Damn, they got me. It's all good, though. I still ain't fuckin' wit' that nigga. I'm on to bigger and better thangs." She poked out her lip, then pushed the visor back up.

"What nigga?" I turned up some *Trey Songz, Jupiter Love* was my cut.

"Lil' Chris, I broke up wit' his ass. Now he got his fat ass sister and her crew sweating me at every turn. I fought that big bitch twice this week already, and for your information, this is her first time getting the better of me. The only reason she did is because I had to fight the other two first."

"Yeah, well, don't do that shit no more because that ain't in yo' best interest." I laughed. "Why that fool Chris can't take you splitting from him?"

She shrugged her shoulders. "Lil' Chris thinks he is God's gift to women, and that he runs everything. He got a crew of dudes that run behind him now after his brother Keeko handed down his Cartel to him. Now Lil' Chris just thinks he can enslave people. He had the nerve to tell me that I was going to be his number two. That I would stay in his trap and have his babies. What? He got me totally misconstrued." She crossed her arms. "Can you take me home?"

I nodded. "I got you." We rolled in silence for a while. It felt awkward. "Yo', I was just playing about all that shit I said back there. You were handling yo' bidness like a true savage. You get mad props for that."

"Thank you." She touched her busted lip again. "Damn, I don't even feel like going home and hearing my dad's mouth. Ever since he's been home, he's been thinking that he can control me like I'm still some little girl. I am eighteen, what part of that doesn't he get?"

I kept rolling, I glanced down at her thick thighs that were encased inside a pair of tight, waist-high jeans. She had gotten a little thicker over the winter, but it looked so good on her. She looked like a younger, finer version of her mother, Jazzy.

"If you want you can come over and chill with me for the night. That way you ain't gotta deal with yo' pops or whatever."

"Yeah, right, I bet you would love that. What, you think I'm some kind of Thot or something?" She looked angry.

"Nah, Shorty, I was just making a suggestion. You said what you didn't wanna do. I was just trying to accommodate you. Offer rescinded."

She was quiet, Trey Songz continued to play on. We were about ten blocks from her apartment. She started to shake her left thigh causing the meat to jiggle. "What are you expecting from me if I spend a night with you? Are you trying to fuck me?"

I laughed. Hell, yeah, I wanted to. I had already got down with her mother so naturally, I wanted to see what the daughter was like between them legs. But I couldn't expose my hand like that. I had to take more of a gentleman approach.

"Tasia, you just got domed fighting three girls. You've been through a lot. I don't mind chilling with you with no strings attached. You bad as hell, but that ain't what I'm on."

"Good because sex is the furthest thing from my brain. I'd be cool to just kick back with you if that's a'ight. Yo' people ain't gon' say nothing?"

"N'all, I got the basement. They don't be coming down there like that." Instead of heading the route to her place, I took the side streets until we got to mine. When I got in the back of the house, I cut the engine. "So, you chillin' wit' me or what?"

She nodded. "Yeah, all I'm asking is that you don't be on that aggressive trying to take nothing bullshit like most not these other Brooklyn niggas. I ain't never heard anything bad about you though, so I trust you."

"Cool den, let's roll inside."

***

"Why I gotta take off my pants in order to get under the covers with you? I thought you said you weren't on that?" Tasia asked standing on the side of the bed with her hand on her hip.

I had already fed her. We smoked a blunt, and now I was trying to swindle her ass into coming out of those pants. Now that I was high, she was looking good as hell to me. My nature was calling out for her.

"I already told you, I wasn't on that. Plus, you already fronting like you trust me anyway." I dusted off the bed. "Come on man."

She was defiant. "You still ain't told me why I need to have my pants off."

"That big girl had you all over the pavement. You know how many germs are on those pants? They all dirty and shit. Plus, who sleeps in their clothes? That's just weird."

She sighed and crossed her arms. "Damn, Tyson, what if I ain't got no damn panties on, then what? Do you think you can still control yourself?"

Hell n'all, if she naked I'm fucking. Ain't no way her thick ass finna lay in my bed all naked and I don't get me some. "You good, Tasia, damn. Look I'll even cut off the lamp." I clicked it off and squeezed my piece under the covers. The television was still on and I could see her clear as day.

"You bet not be on no bullshit." She unbuttoned her pants and hooked her thumbs into the waistband pulling them down.

The TV light flashed bright and I was able to see her trimmed sex lips. She was pudgy down there. She grabbed the sheets, and pulled them back, sliding under the cover with me. I turned the fan on medium.

We just stayed that way for a minute in silence. She rolled on to her side away from me. "You sure ain't nobody gon' come down here and snap out if they catch me?"

I turned on my side and scooted behind her. Her ass molded to my lap. I was expecting her to push me away, but she didn't. I scooted closer and wrapped my arms around her. Her booty was so big and soft.

"I already told you, you're good. Just chill."

"My daddy gets on my nerves. I don't know what prison did to him but ever since he has been home after doing five years, he doesn't act the same. I think I hate him now."

I kissed her shoulder. "Why you say that?"

"Girls got it so hard. We don't really have anybody we can really trust in this world. A man is supposed to protect his daughter. He is supposed to spoil her and treat her like a Princess. She is supposed to be special and off-limits. I wish somebody would tell my father that." She rolled all the way around until she was facing me. "Am I right or am I wrong?"

"You're right." I looked into her eyes and I could tell that she was feeling emotionally sick. "Tasia, you can trust me. Tell me what's really going on."

She looked into my eyes and shook her head. "Is that all males care about, sex?"

"What?"

"N'all, the reason I'm asking you this is because that's how I feel. Ever since I was old enough to know about boys, all they've ever tried to do was sleep with me. I have never been safe around any male, and that's fucked up."

I took my hand off her booty. Suddenly I stopped lusting after her. I wanted to know what her issue was. I sat up and placed my back against the headboard. "I can't speak for no other dude but to me, you're fine as hell. I can't help but think about sex when I look at you because you got all of the parts. I even like them lil' breasts you got."

"That's not the only thing that goes through a female's mind all day and night. We are more emotional, sometimes the best way to get into a woman's pants is by feeding into her emotions and listening to her heart. If you can do that, you will be able to conquer her on a level that most men can't." She sat up beside me. "You brought me here so you could fuck, didn't you?"

The sheets were molded to her thighs. Her legs were slightly spread and all I could think about was the space in between them. Right under that sheet was her naked pussy. That factor was driving me crazy. "Yo', I wanna know what ya pops did to you to have you feeling like you're feeling, right now?"

"Before my daddy went to prison, he was one of the heads of a crew of Dope Boys from out of Harlem that called themselves the Coke Kings. He was revered as a legend. I always heard all these stories when I was a little girl about how amazing he was. I couldn't wait for him to get home so he could spoil me." She stopped, her eyes got bucked. She zoned out for a moment and shook her head to come out of the haze. "Anyway, I don't wanna talk about him. I just want to get some sleep. I've been up for every bit of twelve hours." She slid down the bed and laid on her side. When I didn't move, she looked back at me. "You finna stay up or something?"

I slid down the bed, thought about getting behind her but kept my respective distance. I turned away from her. "Yo', Tasia, I don't know what's been going on with your pops since he got home but I'm here for you if ever you need to talk. I just wanna let you know that." I fluffed my pillow. After it was good and just the way I liked it I laid my head on it and closed my eyes.

"One day I'ma be able to tell you what's really good, Tyson. I can tell you aren't like these other dudes. I just feel it in my heart that you're not." She turned over facing my direction. "Are you mad because we ain't doing nothing?"

"Nah, Goddess, it's good. Everything happens for a reason. Just get you some sleep. It's all love."

She laid there for a moment. Then she leaned over and kissed my cheek. "I owe you one, you'll see. Good night." She rolled back over and fell asleep with me laying a short distance away from her.

I was stuck for a moment. I wondered what her father had done to her to make her feel the way that she was feeling. I could only imagine. All I could tell for sure was that she was hurt and in need of a good friend. I could hear her snoring. I raised the sheets to get one more glance of that fat ass booty and cursed under my breath. That was the dog in me trying to come to the surface. Then the God in me lowered the sheets. I slid behind her and held her protectively.

"I got you, Tasia. I don't know what you are going through but I got you."

Chapter 6

On my eighteenth birthday, my father took it upon himself to whisk me away to Jamaica. He forced me to get up at 3:00 in the morning. By 3:30 we were heading to a Private Jet, and shortly thereafter, we arrived in sunny Kingston, Jamaica with Hermés, and my mother sitting behind me. When the wheels of the Jet screeched on the runway, I had fallen back to sleep and that woke me up. My old man was sitting next to his Jamaican pilot smoking on a Cuban cigar stuffed with some of the best Ganja Kingston had to offer. He turned around and looked back at me.

"Tyson, Mi kno yuh gwine luv di Carnival dat a a tek place fah di nex few days. Deh a nuh oddah way tuh celebrate yuh birtday dan dis. Yuh gwine tank mi fah dis. Truss mi." He blew smoke out of his nostrils before turning back around and conversing with the dread headed pilot.

When we got to the hotel I jumped into the bed and was out like a light. I was so tired that I couldn't keep my eyes open. My mother had this thing that whenever I slept, she liked to rub my back. It had become a comforting tool for both of us ever since I was a baby. She was doing exactly this until I fell asleep. When I woke up three hours later, Hermés was sitting there doing it, and our parents were out of the room.

She smiled down at me. "Yo', lil' dirty ass is finally eighteen. I can only imagine the type of shit daddy got in store for you now. The only reason he ain't been on yo' ass is because mama made him wait until you became a man. Now its curtains. You officially belong to the family's Mafia." She shook her head in sympathy.

I wiped my mouth and sat up. "I don't belong to shit. I'ma do me. I can never see myself following behind no man that shit ain't in the cards." I yawned and stretched my arms over my head.

"Yeah, we gon' see about that. Also, who's been hitting you up back to back like this?" She held up my phone. "I know dis ain't the same Tasia from Brooklyn."

I snatched my phone out of her hand. "Damn, you nosey as a mafucka. Dis is supposed to be my day. It's supposed to be stress-free. You're already giving me a mafuckin' migraine." I scrolled down through the missed calls and read over some of Tasia's text messages.

She was saying she missed me already, and that she had something for me when I got back to New York. I was hoping it was some pussy because although we'd been kicking it for a few months we had yet to do the actual do.

"The only reason I'm asking you this is because Tasia's father is Kammron. Kammron is head of the Coke Kings. Our father is at war with the Coke Kings. I don't know what's going on with them, but as soon as he finds out you're seeing Tasia there is going to be major problems on both sides."

I glared at her. "How do you always know so much shit before I do?"

"Because I got mo' heart than you do. But you'll get there." She stepped into my face, her eyes searched mine. "I love you with all of my heart, Tyson. Whatever daddy about to get you into here, please be safe. I would lose my mind if anything ever happened to you." She kissed me and wrapped her arms around my neck. She hugged me close and laid her head on my chest.

I rubbed her back. "I love you, too. And sooner or later you gon' have to honor my common sense."

My father came into the room as we were hugging. He had my mother behind him. "Tyson, mek wi roll mi waan wi tuh

54

ride fi ah minute before wi celebrate yuh birtday an wollah dat. Cum now bwoy."

***

I don't know where my pops got it from, but I stepped out of the hotel, and we got into a two thousand and eighteen cherry red Hell Cat. He jumped into the driver's seat, and I slid into the passenger's. He dropped the top and pulled a Draco from the back seat placing it on his lap. A black Chevy Astro van pulled beside us and stopped. A dark-skinned man with dreads and a hooped earring hanging from his nose looked down at my pops.

"Follow us. Any bombaclat luk funny, yuh lick shot fos an ask questions neva."

The dark-skinned man nodded and allowed us to roll off before he pulled behind us. There was another van in front of us. My pops had security on point. I sat back with my arm on the windowsill of the car. It was hot and humid, but there was a slight breeze while we were in traffic that felt just right.

"Yuh mite ave bin baan eena Brooklyn son buh dis place yah a unnu yaad. Dis a di island dat runs tru unnu veins Nah di odda one yuh madda a fram. Jamrock a di center addi di wurl."

I squinted my eyes from the sun. We were rolling past the beach and there were so many gorgeous and thick chocolate women walking along the sand that I couldn't focus on nothing he was saying. My eyes were like a kid in a candy shop.

He popped me. "Focus bwoy! Deh will bi time fah wollah dat latah. Fah now yuh muss listen tuh dees words. ."

I rubbed my shoulder. "What words, Pops?"

"Now dat yuh a eighteen, mi haffi staat a get yuh ready tuh step up as di prince addi Mafia. Yuh a fi mi so-so son. Di throne will bi handed dung tuh yuh."

I nodded my head. "You making it seem like I don't even have a choice. What if I don't want to be a prince of our family's Mafia?"

He looked at me with bloodshot red eyes. "Den mi will kill yuh by cutting yuh ed aff yuh nek." He mugged me with intense hatred.

I swallowed as I imagined him doing everything that he had threatened. It made me feel a way. I didn't like nobody to make decisions for me. I was my own man and I knew I could never run behind my father or nobody else. I had to be the one in charge, even if I didn't know for sure what I was going to be in charge of as of yet.

My Pops kept rolling. "Wi bout tuh buck up wid ah circle ah bosses. Deadly mon dat run di island an major parts addi wurl. Yuh will nah embarrass mi. Yuh will casco eh until yuh mek ih."

"Sounds cool, I just hate that we gotta do all of this on my birthday. Why we can't do it tomorrow or somethin'?" I was irritated.

Jamaica was known for having some of the baddest African women in the world. I wanted to explore them. I was a fresh eighteen, and the world was set to be my oyster.

"Bikaaz wi a a duh dis todeh. Ah birtday a ongle ah day. Yuh will git unnu bly tuh celebrate bai ah dem dem way dat yuh need tuh. Buh yuh fos one belongs tuh jamrock.."

"Den I guess it's settled then. I mean what's the use of me having my own thoughts if you're going to decide my life for me anyway. I might as well give you a controller, and hook it up to my back and let you do what you do because—"

Smack!

King of the Trap

My pops backhanded me so fast that I spit blood across the windshield. He took his Draco and aimed the barrel toward me. "Yuh cum fram fi mi balls, buh mi swear tuh di heavens dat mi will put ah hundred shots eena yuh bitch. Yuh respeck di game An yuh respeck mi. Yuh taak dat taak an lose yuh life. Mia di negus. Dat a wah dem call mi here; dat a wah mia. Yuh 'ear mi, bwoy?"

I tasted my own blood, held the corners of my mouth while I mugged him with hatred. "Yeah, Pops, I hear you." My eyes gazed down to the Draco pointed at me.

"Aright den. Wen wi git 'ear yuh shut up, an pay attention. Biznizz fos, den pleasure. ." He repositioned the Draco and stepped on the gas, after passing me a fat blunt of Kingston's finest.

✳✳✳

An hour later we were in the middle of the sea floating on a big Yacht that was filled with angry-looking Jamaicans, both men, and women. Each Cartel or Mafia seemed to have security with them. You could tell the difference in each bosses' security because of their style of dress, and their colors. My pop's security wore all black. Half of their faces were also covered by masks, and if their dreads weren't down to their waist, he wasn't hiring them.

They looked angry, hungry, and high off a bunch of drugs. Their eyes were bloodshot red, and each man held a weapon. They surrounded me and my old man ready to murder anything that looked out of place. There were other crews there that looked just as vicious.

Forty minutes after we were on the Yacht my father came to me and placed his arm around my neck. "Ih turns out dat yuh nuh need tuh bi present fah di meeting, buh before wi hab

57

ih, di Queen waah tuh buck up yuh.—" He paused. He smelled like Old Spice and Ganja. He turned so that he was looking me in the eyes. "Shi a di most important ooman eena wollah jamrock. Yuh treat har wid di ultimate respeck Ar wi will bi forced tuh gwaana war wid all dees powerful people dat yuh si 'ear. Am mi a mek miself clear?"

"I got you, Pop."

"Good, come."

He guided me inside the living room of the Yacht. Before we entered, we had to be approved by eight, big muscle bound security guards that had thick dreads down to their waists. We passed them, and it became cool. The interior of the Yacht must've had the air-conditioning blowing on high. It felt like wintertime. We navigated through two rooms before we found the Queen. She was sitting in an old-style Wicker chair blowing a Ganja stuffed cigar. She was dark-skinned, with gray eyes, and dreads that fell to the floor. She had a bunch of gold rings on her fingers. When she saw me, she smiled briefly and then frowned. There were three heavily armed guards behind her.

My father came and bowed in front of her. "Fi mi Queen Mi brought fi mi seed fah unnu blessing an di blessing ah jamrock." He turned and waved me over.

I slowly came to him, he forced me to one knee. I damn near twisted my ankle getting to the floor. Once there I mugged my Pops. He glared at me and I lowered my head.

The Queen leaned forward and gripped my head inside her little hand. "Yuh ave nuh chrent pan unnu scalp. Bald headed lakka ah bombaclat. Weh a unnu mane?"

I was quiet. My pops smacked me in the back of the head. "Ansah har, bwoy!"

"It's growing, I'll have it soon." I didn't even know if I wanted dreads.

I was the type of dude that liked to stay groomed. Dreads seemed very messy and unclean to me. Plus, I didn't know how they would make me look?

"Ah man's chrent a nuh so-so eena fi im muscles buh also eena fi im locks. All di leaders eena jamrock hab locks Ar dem a stripped ah fi dem slots. Yuh young an healthy." She pinched my cheeks, and slid her finger around in my mouth, pulling open my lips. She tapped on my teeth. "Very healthy. Yuh need locks bwoy Den yuh can bi criss lakka yuh daadie Negus." She looked down at him. My pops kept his head lowered.

"Yes ma'am," was my only reply.

"Dis bwoy a very handsome, Negus. Mi tink he a ah criss fit fah Ashlynn, afta all.." She mused, looking down at my old man.

My pops looked up. "Eff ih bi suh, mi will akcep an suh will he har hand eena marriage.."

"*Marriage?*" I looked over at my father.

He took the back of my head and stuffed it to the floor. "Unnu blessing fi, mi Queen."

She nodded. I saw this when I glanced upward. She took a long stick and began to whack me on the back while she chanted. The whacks weren't hard enough to cause serious pain, but I felt them. When she finished, she grabbed my ears and kissed my lips hard. "Ashlynn."

My father smiled. "Ashlynn."

I didn't know what that word meant but for some reason, it gave me chills. I felt like they had some kind of secret going on that involved me, but I wasn't a part of it. It made me feel like a slave. I felt trapped and afraid of what was to come.

Even though it was supposed to be my birthday I couldn't focus on anything other than trying to find out what that Ashlynn word meant. Hermés didn't know what it meant and neither did my mother. My father wouldn't tell me and that pissed me off. Instead of going out that night and enjoying myself, I stayed inside the hotel room with the covers pulled over my head. I told the family, I didn't want to be bothered and they granted my wish.

Chapter 7

"Tyson! Tyson! Wake yo' monka ass up now boy!" My father King yelled from the middle of the hotel room.

I pulled the blanket from over my head and looked out at him with a hazy vision, and anger surging through me. "Pop, what up man?" I didn't feel like dealing with him under any circumstances.

I was already feeling shitty because I had squandered my special day away that was meant for me. So, after spending a few hours talking on the phone with Tasia, I'd decided to take a nap. Now here was my father calling me like I had done something wrong.

He stepped closer to the bed with Ganja smoke coming out of both of his nostrils. "Get yo' monka ass up. We got bidness ta tend to, right now."

I sat up and rubbed my fists over my eyes. "Yo' Pop, I just wanna chill, B. I ain't feeling dis whole Jamaica scene, word is bond I miss Brooklyn."

My Pops stood there for a second puffing on his blunt. He blew smoke out of his mouth and tilted his head back toward the ceiling. "Tyson, yuh get ten minutes tuh buck up mi downstairs. Mi nah gwine ramp wid yuh bout dis yah biznizz. Git up!" He threw open the hotel room door and stepped into the hallway where three of his big security guards were waiting for him. They closed the door behind him.

I sat on the edge of the bed feeling like snapping out. I had to break away from King. I didn't like being under his control, and I didn't like anybody telling me what to do. I jumped out of the bed in my boxers and started getting dressed when Hermés came out of the bathroom with a towel wrapped around her. She clicked her tongue against her teeth and shook her head. I mugged her.

"I don't know why you looking at me like that. I ain't the one that ruined your sleep, Daddy is." She walked up to me and stood in my face. "Kid, he's about to have you show out for these Jamaican mafuckas. I know for a fact that when you come back you are going to have some blood on your hands. Mark my words."

I fastened my pants and looked up at her. "What you think his old ass on?"

"The Jamaicans look at him as if he really is some sort of King. You best believe he will not allow you to embarrass him. He's gonna want you to shed blood, and you're going to have to do it in such a way. Trust me on this."

I nodded my head in preparation. "You know what sis, I'm to the point that I don't even give a fuck anymore. I'm just gon' do the shit that he wants me to do here so we can get back to Brooklyn. When we get back there, I'm moving the fuck out of his house and I'm finna get my shit out the mud." I threw my shirt over my body. "Fuck Jamaica, I ain't never coming back to dis mafucka." I got ready to leave out of the door once I had my shoes on. I wiggled my foot inside of them. I was a bit worried about what my Pops had set up for me.

Hermés blocked my path and looked into my eyes. She rested her hands on my chest. "Lil' bruh, be careful out there. I know I say dis all the time, but I really mean it. If anything ever happens to you I would lose my fuckin' mind. I'm already on the verge of going insane. I need you can you please understand that?"

I tried to calm myself down. My Pops had me vexed. "Yeah, I understand that, sis."

"Good." She smiled looking at me for what seemed like a long time, then she kissed and hugged me tightly.

***

When I got downstairs my father was standing on the side of a black on black Hummer. He moved to the side, and I slid into the passenger's seat. His bodyguard closed the door behind me. My Pops walked around and got into the driver's seat. Once there he handed me a Mach. 90.

"Yuh still memba how tuh lick shot one ah dees, rite?" He asked this with a smirk on his face.

"Yeah, I do. What's going on?" I wanted to know because he had all those security guards that were trained to kill. Why would he ever need me to raise a gun to do anything? That didn't make any sense to me.

He started up the Hummer and pulled off into the cool Jamaican night. "Tonite a di nite dat yuh earn di Prince's crown. Yuh will conquer Manifest an earn Ashlynn." He popped open his ashtray and handed me the blunt that was sitting inside of it. It was so fat that it looked like a regular cigar before it was busted down.

"That's another thing; who the hell is Ashlynn? And now you're saying Manifest. What is that a person or a mission?" I pushed in the Hummer's lighter.

My Pops rolled for a moment, then pointed at the lighter when it clicked back out. He waited until I sparked the blunt before he took it from me and began to puff on it emitting big clouds of smoke into the Hummer. "Ashlynn a unnu prize An Manifest a unnu mission. Before wi cut jamrock, yuh will finish Manifest an obtain Ashlynn. Deh a nuh way roun ih." He took three more pulls off the blunt and passed it to me.

I puffed trying to wrap my head around things. I didn't like the fact that he was talking to me as if he was speaking in a riddle. I wanted to snap and say something slick about how he was acting like a scary-ass nigga for not coming right out and saying what he had to say, but I decided against it.

"You know what, King?" I ran my tongue across my teeth and sucked them. "I'ma do whatever you need me to do tonight, but when we get back to New York I'm moving out of your crib and branching off so I can do my own thing. I ain't with this slavery stuff that you got me going through."

"*Slavery?* bwoy yuh cyaan begin tuh undastan wah eh really feels lakka tuh bi eena slavery. Mi did ah eena eh ah time aguh an yuh cudda nebba survived ih. Truss mi pan dat. Dis yah a mi throwing yuh ah bone. Helping yuh git tuh weh yuh need tuh bi inna game. Yuh cyaan even tek wah deh a bi offered tuh yuh an shut up bout ih."

"Yo' you my Pops, King. Word to Jehovah man, if you was anybody else you would never be able to talk to me like you doing right now."

My Pops looked at me and kept rolling. He turned some Reggae music on the speakers and started to nod his head. "Fi mi pupa nebba did gi mi a chance lakka mi giving yuh. Yuh back talk Yuh mek faces. Any ah dat deh an mi would've bin dead inna ocean. Yuh luddy mi gi yuh as bai chances as mi duh.."

I scoffed. "Like I said, I'ma do whatever you want me to do tonight but when we get back to New York I'ma do my own thing." I didn't know exactly what that was going to be, but it had to be better than whatever this was. I felt like a prisoner. My Pops made me feel like I was nothing more than a robot. I hated him at times because of that.

"Fi as lang as yuh liv, an yuh ave fi mi blood flowing tru yuh veins, yuh will eva deh duh wah mi tell yuh tuh duh. Eeda dat ar buck up death. Mi created yuh an mi wi kill yuh an figet yuh did evah existed. Mi mean dat shit.." He mugged me, then turned back to driving down the highway along the dark ocean that looked eerie and dark.

I didn't respond to those words that had come from his mouth. There was nothing I could say. King was powerful. King had an army of savages that followed behind him. Savages that would kill on his command. He was used to getting whatever he wanted in the game. The fact that I was a defiant son messed with his pride. I got that. What I didn't get was why he thought he would always be able to control me.

Then on top of that, he made it perfectly clear that whenever I stopped listening to his orders or allowing him to run things that he would kill me. This only told me that I needed to get my priorities in order. I had to get my weight up in the game. If I chose to stay passive, then my pops would always rule over me with the threat of death. But when I allowed myself to man up, and stand on my own two feet, only then could I take back my life. I was eighteen, a man. There was no more room for me to be treated like or claimed as a kid. I was a grown man, and I needed to stand up like one.

"Tonite a di nite yuh a guh shed blood fah di crown as fi mi Prince. Fi im name a Manifest. He a di fos son ah Garvey. Garvey a ed addi Deadly Gorillas yah eena Kingston. Dem a fi wi family's worst enemy. Fi wi beef date all to how bac tuh di early nineteen-hundreds. Eh a ah lesson fi anedda day. Tonite Manifest muss drop out during di Carnival. Yuh muss shed fi im blood an implant yuhself widin di soil ah jamrock. Am mi clear?"

I was a little scared because I didn't know shit about what my Pops was talking about, but at the same time, I was ready to get this shit over with. "I'm ready Pops just tell me what I need to do."

***

The Jamaican Carnival was still jumping at two in the morning. Most of the locals still had on their masks, or paint all over their faces to celebrate the festival. Loud music serenaded the streets with drummers beating on their percussions, or trumpet players blowing their horns as loud as they could. The females were still dancing as if they were hopped up on some drug and trying their best to get the twerking out of their system because they left the party. The scent of Ganja was loud in the air, along with perfume and Cologne. The salt from the sea mixed with all the aromas to create the fragrance of freedom.

My face was painted all black like the attire I was now wearing. I had a dreadlock wig on that allowed the fake locks to fall to my waist. It was a cool night, but hot enough for the women to be wearing the bare minimum like they were. I could feel the .9 millimeter in my lower back as I eased through the crowd like a hunter. My stomach continued to do somersaults, yet I was laser-focused on the mission at hand.

Twenty steps, nineteen-eighteen-seventeen-sixteen. I got closer and closer to Manifest as he stood with his back to the direction that I was coming up from. In front of him was a light-skinned female dancing in his lap. Even from the distance that I was, I could see that she also had long dreads and a voluptuous figure. Manifest swayed to the left, and then the right.

Eight steps, seven steps, six steps, five. My eyes lowered, sweat rolled down my back. I just needed to get this shit over with. I was scared I ain't gon' even lie.

A female ran in front of Manifest suddenly and screamed at the top of her lungs pointing at him. The crowd seemed to stop all at once to see what the issue was. I could hear the murmurings all around me.

Four steps, three-two-one.

"Say, Manifest!" I hollered pulling the gun out of the small of my back.

He turned around to face me and squinted his eyes. Then he hung his mouth wide open. I stepped forward and started shooting. The first three bullets ripped his face in half. He slumped to the ground and laid twisted. Screams came from all around. I stood over him and shot him ten more times, before running through the crowd. All the people were running in every direction creating pandemonium. My heart was beating faster and faster until I jumped back in the Hummer and my father pulled off.

He had an evil smile on his face. "Mi proud, bwoy. Mia very, very proud." He pointed over his shoulder toward the back seat. "Sumady ready tuh buck up yuh."

I looked over my shoulder still trying to catch my breath. I couldn't believe I had killed somebody. I was seconds away from freaking out. Especially when I saw the female sitting in the back seat that had been standing in front of and dancing with Manifest. I was confused.

"Son, buck up, Ashlynn. Ashlynn, yuh nuh langa belong tuh Manifest ar di Deadly Guerillas. Dis a yuh Prince now, an yuh belong tuh dis fambily. Undastan?"

She nodded her head with tears running down her cheeks. "Yes, King, mi undastan."

Now I was more confused than ever. I had so many questions. I was so lost, I felt so sick. I kept seeing Manifest's murder in my mind's eye. It was haunting to me, and what was Ashlynn's importance in all of this. My head was spinning like a Merry Go Round. I needed my sister, I was sure she would explain everything.

That night when I got back to the hotel, Hermés, was sitting on the edge of the bed waiting for me. I came inside and took my shirt off, dropping the gun to the floor. She got out of the bed and picked it up with plastic gloves already on her hands. She made sure that it was empty and took the clip out of it, setting everything on the dresser.

"You killed Manifest tonight, didn't you?"

I nodded my head and took a deep breath. "Yeah."

She nodded and hugged my body. "Then it is done."

"What are you talking about? What is done?" I wanted to know, I needed to.

"Everything will be explained to you in time, but what you just did has cemented our family at the top of the totem pole 'ear inn jamrock. Dad can now say that he is the rightful King because he has a living heir, and Garvey cannot. You're locked in now, Tyson. I'm so sorry." She wrapped her arms around me and held me tightly.

I hugged her more afraid than I have ever been. My muscles tensed. I felt cold, I was lost. There were no words that could be spoken from me. Instead of talking, I chose to hold Hermés through the night, until I was able to fall to sleep.

Chapter 8

I don't know how it happened, or why it happened but it was a hot Friday afternoon when my father King, and fifty of his animals loaded me, Hermés, and my mother into a small shack-like church inside of Kingston. I stood at the front of the church dressed in a black and white tuxedo that my Pops had to threaten me to step into. Sweat peppered along the edges of my forehead. I was shaking and my fists were balled tight. I glanced over at Hermés, and she mouthed the words that she was sorry. My mother looked straight ahead in silence. She appeared to be in a somber mood. The wedding music began to play by a short, fat, dark-skinned Jamaican sitting at the Organ. I took a deep breath and tried to calm myself as I watched the door.

Ashlynn appeared dressed in a white and opaque wedding dress, the veil covered her face. My father walked her down the aisle step by step until she was standing beside me smelling like Jasmine perfume. I turned to her and pulled the veil back. Her face was a ball of anger. She shot daggers into my eyes before she looked over at my father and softened. She reached out for my hands and I gave them to her shivering at first touch. I didn't want to do this.

My father stepped in front of us and read all the usual wordings from the Bible when it came to weddings. Then he got to the part where I began to feel like I was about to throw up. "Ashlynn, do ya promise tuh love Tyson through thick and thin, rich and poor, sick and in health as long as yuh two shall live?"

Ashlynn was quiet for a moment. She gathered a few breaths, closed her eyes, and slowly opened them back. "I will."

"And Tyson, do you swear to do dee same. Ya heard di last words. Yes or no?"

"I really don't know you, Shorty, but this here is bigger than me, so I guess I will."

King took a step forward as if he was ready to attack me. He stopped after looking over at my mother. "By dee pow-wah vested in me, you two are married until deaf. Kiss huh, son."

I wanted to get the shit over with, so I grabbed Ashlynn and gave her a quick peck on her lips. She was cold as a snowball. She tensed and scrunched her face. After the kiss was over, she wiped her mouth and looked in the chapel as if she was expecting somebody to appear. When she couldn't locate them, her shoulders sunk, she looked defeated.

The celebration was small but appropriate for the occasion. I couldn't allow myself to get too caught up in what was going on. I wanted to get out of Jamaica, I missed New York, I missed Brooklyn. To be honest I missed Tasia. Being around Ashlynn made me think about her every second of every day, and that was rare for me. I was wondering what she was doing while I was forced to marry Ashlynn.

I imagined Tasia spending time with another man and it made me want to go berserk. I took one look over at my mother. We made eye contact for a moment before she looked me off and disappeared out of the church. I found a seat and took it lowering my head wishing I could've been anywhere else other than where I was. I spent the rest of the celebration right in that chair.

***

That night when we got back to the hotel my father had arranged it so that Ashlynn and I had our own room to share.

He insisted that we consummate our marriage. As soon as me and Ashlynn were inside the room with the door closed she ripped her wedding gown from her body and slammed it to the ground.

"There if you want me, you're going to have to come and kill me. I will never submit to you, Tyson. Never!" She turned a bright shade of red and balled her fists. Underneath her wedding dress, she wore just a white bra and panty set.

"Shorty what the fuck is wrong with you? I don't want yo' lil' yellow ass either. You ain't even my type." I picked up her dress and threw it at her. "You can put that shit back on."

She caught it and threw it back to the ground. She took three steps toward me. "You killed Manifest! You dirty murderer! I will kill you in honor of him." Her chest heaved up and down. Her eyes were watery. Her fists were balled tight.

I took a step back and really looked at her. She was gorgeous, and the madder she appeared the finer she looked to me. She also appeared crazy.

I held my hands out in front of me. "Look, Shorty, I don't know what you're talking about but I ain't did shit. I don't even know this Manifest nigga that you talking about. I'm from Brooklyn."

"You're a liar. I was born and raised in Kingston. I understand and get the legend. You are the first-born son of King Jean. Manifest is the first-born son of Garvey Petwa. Garvey and your father have been at each other's necks since they were in the eighth-grade and King took your mother away from Garvey. Both King and Garvey are from the merciless jungles of Jamaica. They each are widely respected and revered. Both men have built up deadly Guerilla Killas that flood the Americas with narcotics, and they slay their competition with sinister killings. Both men were set to be king of Jamaica, but a man is not eligible to be king if he has no living heir. The legend says that in order to be king one's heir must slay the weaker heir, only then can that man be king. Your father brought you down here to Jamaica to slay Manifest. Admit it!" She stepped into my face.

I backed up once again. I now had a firm understanding as to what was going on. It was as Hermés had said. My father had me in the middle of some bullshit. "Look, I ain't killed nobody and I ain't trying to be Prince of nothing. I'ma school nigga. I don't know what is going on down here on the island but it ain't got shit to do with me." I sidestepped her.

She grabbed my arm and turned me around. "Manifest and I come from the same slums. We took baths in puddles of mud since we were little children. He understood me. He knew where I came from and the pains associated with it. How could you kill him?" Tears seeped out of her eyes.

I frowned, and rushed her little ass, pinning her against the wall. "Bitch, didn't I say I ain't have shit to do with that, huh?"

She fought against me to no avail. "Let me go."

"Fuck that." I held her tighter. "You steady talking this dumb shit. I ain't killed no mafuckin' body. I been enjoying my vacation. Whatever my Pops got going on is his business. I ain't on that. You hear me, huh?" I pushed her into the wall hard and let her go.

She fell to her knees crying her eyes out. "Why is this happening?" She rocked back and forth. Her sobbing became louder and louder.

I watched her from a distance. I paced back and forth. The sound of her crying was getting the better of me. I always hated to hear the audio of a crying female. It did something to my spirit, it weakened me. I came over and kneeled beside her. My hand hovered over her back before I brought it down.

She jerked away from me and stood up. She backed all the way up to the wall with her eyes wide open. "Why me? Why did your father King choose me for you? Why not another girl, huh? Why me!" She screamed.

I stood up. "I don't know. I don't know what the fuck is going on down here."

"Is it because of my royal bloodline? My Father Damien? Well, he abandoned us and left us for dead while he stayed in mansions in Miami back in the States. I hated him, and a brutal death was his karma. Just you watch." She came from the wall and wiped her tears with that back of her hands.

"Like I said I don't know what is going on here. I'm just vacationing. I ain't got shit to do wit' Manifest being killed. I ain't heard nothin' about my Pops doing that shit either or his animals. You spitting a whole lot of accusations with no facts. Where I am from that shit will get you killed."

"Then kill me and let me be free to soar with Manifest. I will never submit to you the murderer. Your karma will be by the sword of your own doing. Mark those cursed words." She turned her back to me. Her ass had swallowed her panties. It looked like she was wearing a thong.

"So, what are we going to do then, huh? You gon' hold a grudge against me for some shit I didn't do? Is that fair? Well, in case you haven't noticed we are fucking married. You are my wife now. We gotta get this shit together because all this is beyond us. Get that through your head."

She ran her hands over her face. "I am so miserable. I curse this beauty of mine. This yellow skin in Jamaica has always been a problem. Outside I am gorgeous. On the inside, I am the ugliest woman in all the islands combined. I am sick." She fell to her knees. "Where is Odana?"

"*Odana*, who is that?"

She looked up at me with glossy eyes. "Odana is my fifteen-year-old sister. She is all that I have left after our mother passed away two years ago. I won't go to the states with a man that has murdered my best friend, and whose family is responsible for the disappearance of Odana. Kill me now, I welcome the Reaper."

Damn this chick was screwed up. What made it so bad was that she was now my wife. I felt more lost than a kid's mitten at recess. "Shorty, I don't know any Odana. And I am not responsible for her disappearance. I can help you to find her, but I swear this isn't on me."

"Your father says Odana will come to America along with my submission." She lowered her head. "What is life?"

I stood looking down on her wanting to comfort her so bad. I could see that she was hurting. Even though I didn't know her like that I still wanted to heal her. "I thought Manifest was your boyfriend or your fianceé. You just said that he was your best friend only."

She ran her fingers through her reddish-brown tresses. "I never said only." She sighed. "Manifest wasn't into women. He preferred men and I think that is why it was so easy for the elders of the island to agree to have him killed. They couldn't allow the Prince of the island to be a gay man even if his father Garvey is head of the Deadly Guerillas." She began to cry again. "He was such a good man. Kindhearted, strong, sincere, and he would give anybody the shirt off their back. And you killed him."

"But that is the thing, I didn't. I didn't even know this Manifest person. I didn't have anything against him. You have to believe that." I knew I was lying but damn she had me feeling horrible. I was experiencing a sudden case of remorse the more she spoke about Manifest.

"It will take a lot for you to prove that you didn't kill him. For now, I believe what I believe. Nobody can change that." She curled on her side on the floor and began to sing a song just loud enough for me to hear her.

I couldn't understand the words because she spoke them in French, but the more she sang the harder she cried.

That night I laid in bed dazed and lost. I didn't understand fully what my father was up to, but I hated him for the depths that he'd involved me. I just wanted to live a normal life. I didn't want to be involved in crime. I didn't ever want to kill anybody. Answering to another man all the time was even worse, even if that man was my father King. I needed to find a way to break away from him, and his Rasta Mafia, even if it meant I would place myself under the gun. Freedom would be worth it.

T.J. Edwards

Chapter 9

We arrived back in New York City two days later after me and Ashlynn were made to stay cooped up inside our hotel room the entire time. We never consummated our marriage, and I had no desire to. I wanted to get the hell out of Jamaica. It was a bright and sunny day full of blue skies when the Private Jet's wheels screeched on the runway and began to bring the small plane to a halt. I could see the skyline of the city and my stomach turned over a few times in anticipation. There was no place in the world like New York City, and in my opinion, Brooklyn was the best borough.

As soon as the limousine pulled up in front of my parent's house, I jumped out of it, ran into the middle of the street of our block, and kissed the ground three times. I was home and I felt like crying. When I looked back at the limo Ashlynn was stepping out of it with her long, curly hair blowing behind her. She blocked her eyes from the harsh sunlight and scanned the busy neighborhood until she found me kneeled on the ground. She grabbed her suitcase out of the limo and held it in her right hand.

I came over and took it from her, after being in the room for two days straight together we'd managed to come to an understanding that we weren't each other's enemies. I was sure I had convinced her that I hadn't been the one that killed Manifest. She became slightly warmer toward me, and I was thankful for that. Her Hazel eyes sparkled in the sunlight.

"You okay?"

"Your father says that he will be bringing Odana over in a few weeks. I am so excited. He wants us to get pregnant right away, though. That makes me sick." She lowered her head.

I wrapped my arm around her waist. The block was packed. It looked like the entire neighborhood was outside.

There were door boys out washing their cars. There were also a bunch of females doing this all up and down the block as well. Children were spraying water guns. Girls were screaming while they were being chased. Little boys were playing football in the middle of the street, while others had nailed a crate to the light pole and were playing basketball on it. A bunch of little girls were playing hopscotch and double Dutch. I smelled barbecue being cooked as well. This was Brooklyn.

Something told me to look across the street, and when I did, I spotted her. Tasia was coming down the steps from one of her many girlfriends' houses. When she saw me, she went into a trance-like state. She came down each step slowly with her eyes trained on me, she tripped and stumbled from being so focused and came down the rest of the stairs until she was on the sidewalk.

"Tyson." She came into the street coming directly for me.

I released Ashlynn and headed toward her. We met in the middle of the street.

"Tyson," she repeated.

I opened my arms wide and allowed her to walk into them. She hugged me, and I returned her hug with my eyes closed. She felt so warm and perfect. "I missed you, Tasia. I can't even lie about that right there."

"It feels like you've been gone for a whole year. There is so much bullshit that has happened since you've been gone. My father has gotten worse." She lowered her voice when she said this last part.

I came out of our embrace just a little bit so I could look into her face. I held both sides of it with my hands. The sunlight beamed off her brown skin. Her almond eyes were squinted to protect her from its harmful rays.

"We need to chill together. Seriously, what do you have going on tonight?"

Before she could respond my father walked up to us with his arm around Ashlynn's neck. He sort of nudged me out of the way so he could stand directly in Tasia's face. "Tasia, it's good tuh see you. Meet my daughter in law and Tyson's wife. Her name is Ashlynn."

Tasia winced, bucked her eyes, and looked over at me. "*Wife?* You went down there and got married? Why didn't you tell me, Tyson?"

I mugged my father. He had an amused look on his face. If he wasn't my pops I would've cold-cocked his ass. "Yo', I can explain everything. That's why we need to get together tonight."

Tasia backed up and looked over to Ashlynn. Tasia shook her head. "Nall, forget this. Y'all are all alike, I swear all you men are just alike. You're just dogs." She backed into the street and walked back to her friend's place. She took one final glance before she ran up the stoop, and into the Walk-Up Complex.

I watched her disappear. "Pops, why would you do that? Why wouldn't you allow me to tell her all this on my own? You had no right."

King laughed. "What's done is done? Come on, it's time dat you cater to her wife. Tasia comes from enemy bloodline. If eva it comes down to war she would be nothing more than a casualty. Let's go." He kissed Ashlynn on the cheek and headed up the stairs into our Walk-Up Complex with Ashlynn following behind him.

My mother Amanda walked up to me and kissed my cheek. "I can tell that you really like that Tasia girl. If you want her bad enough you will find a way to get her. Love conquers all things. You are a man now. Soon your wisdom will overtake you. Your heart will want what it desires, and nobody will be able to prevent you from having what you crave. Search for your inner Lion, it is there my son. I love you." She kissed my cheek again and walked up the stairs with her golden curly hair flowing behind her.

I stood right there on the sidewalk looking over at Tasia's friend's house. I wanted to go over there so bad and talk to her. I felt like I needed to explain how I really felt about her, and Ashlynn. Because my father was denying me her, I found myself yearning for Tasia in a way that I never had before. I continued to look at the Walk-Up. A curtain on the upstairs window of Tasia's friend's building moved to the side. Suddenly Tasia was visible. We locked eyes. That was the only sign that I needed. I got ready to head across the street when King came out of the house and called my name.

"Tyson, your wife needs you."

I paused mid-step and sighed. "Damn, Pop." My eyes looked back up to the window where Tasia had been but now she was gone.

***

"So, I guess that was your girlfriend, huh?" Ashlynn asked me after we'd finished eating one of my mother's famous West Indies meals.

I had picked over my food. I didn't have an appetite. All I could think about was Tasia. "N'all, we just cool but I feel a way for her, though. I can't even lie about that." I sat on the edge of my bed in the basement. On the table was one of Tasia's scrunchies that she'd left behind. I wretched and held my stomach.

Ashlynn shook her head. "It looks like it's more than that. Seems to me that you love this girl. I bet you feel like shit for marrying me now, huh?" She sat on the bed next to me. I could smell her perfume, I didn't like it.

"If it was up to me, I wouldn't be married to nobody. I'm only eighteen, and I ain't got a pot to piss in. I ain't worthy to be married to no woman. Not even you." I laid on my back and looked up at the ceiling. Damn, I missed Tasia.

"What do you mean, not even me? You don't even know me to automatically write me off as unworthy to be wed to. Besides your little girlfriend didn't look like she was all of that. The men in Jamaica wouldn't give her a second glance." She looked down at me.

I sat up feeling offended. "Why because she isn't yellow like you? Because she doesn't have those Hazel eyes and that good hair?" I did air quotes with my fingers. "I don't give a fuck what those niggas down there would think. In my opinion the darker the woman the more beautiful. The kinkier the natural hair the sexier. Tasia is a sistah in every sense of the word. Fuck those Rastafarian mafuckas, word up."

"Aw, so because I'm light-skinned that makes me less attractive? Because my hair is naturally curly, and my eyes flip from hazel to green that makes me less of a sistah." She scoffed. "How about you say screw your own opinions instead of casting them my way for the negative. Have you ever thought about that?"

"Man shut the fuck up. You talk too much. You making me wanna bust you in that mafucka." I stood up and hovered over her.

She stood up. "What you think I'ma do if you hit me in my mouth? Do you think I'm just going to sit back and do nothing?" She balled her fists.

"Man." I pushed her lil' ass on the bed so hard that she flew into the middle of it.

She bounced twice and wound up on her side. She scooted out of the bed and swung to slap me across the face. Hermés had me way more than prepared for an attack as such. I ducked and wrapped my arms around her.

"Let me go you bombaclat New Yorker. Get your filthy mitts off me right this minute."

I kept holding her. I clutched my muscles and squeezed just a tad. She groaned, I loosened my grip a bit. "Ashlynn, I'm sorry for what I said if you felt any sort of disrespect. I apologize for pushing you to. That was uncalled for. You're not my enemy, I'm just mad right now." I released her.

She pushed me hard and guarded her face as if she was getting ready for me to attack her. "Don't you ever put your hands on me, American. I will kill you if you do."

"Man shut up." I waved her lil' yellow ass off. I sat on the bed and lowered my head. "Damn this is some bullshit."

She slowly lowered her guard. She came and sat beside me. "I feel sick, Tyson. Your father told me that the only way he is going to allow me and Odana to be together again is when I get pregnant by you. He craves a grandchild that will come from my womb. I'm so depressed I don't know what to do."

I don't know why I did it, but I put my arm around her shoulder. I rested my head against hers. "Looks like we are both in a fucked up position. The last thing we need to do is be fighting each other. I don't have anything against you. I know you are hurting because of Manifest and Odana. If there is any way I can help you to feel better please tell me and I will do my absolute best to be there for you. After all, you are my wife."

"Yeah, I guess I really am." She was quiet, and so was I.

We didn't say a word for five or so minutes.

She finally stood up and turned to face me. "So, how are we going to do this?"

I glanced up at her. "Do what?"

"This marriage. Are we going to slowly transition into actually being in a relationship with each other, or are we going to fight against the process the entire time?" She kneeled in front of me. "The reason I ask is because King Locust has a reputation for impatience. He will only give me so long before he dismisses me as your wife, and has both me and Odana killed. He is a shady man as I am sure you are aware. I think we need to be smart."

"And what does smart for you look like?" I so desperately needed her to shed wisdom on things because I was more lost than ever. I didn't have a clue what I was getting ready to do.

"Being smart is taking it until we make it. I am willing to be impregnated if it means that I will get my sister back. I am also willing to give you a chance as my husband because the Bible makes it very clear that after a woman is married to a man her only release from him should be under death. If she is to leave under any other circumstances she will forever be cursed with unhappiness and torment." She walked away, taking my hands in her own. "Tyson, I am willing to be your wife. We both have an agenda, and I'm okay with that. What do you say?"

Her fingers were soft and warm. Looking down into her eyes started to make me feel a way. She was gorgeous. There was no denying that. But deep in my heart of hearts, I could feel that she wasn't for me. My phone vibrated. I needed that distraction. I stood up and grabbed it off the dresser. Tasia's face was on it. I trembled.

The bottom read, *//: We need to talk. Come over tonight, 1:00 a.m.*

Giddily, I texted back immediately, *//: I'll be there.* Then I put my phone back on the dresser.

Ashlynn stood up. "Who was that?"

"Nobody. Now, what were you saying?"

She crossed her arms, smacked her lips, and rolled her eyes. "What are we going to do about us? We have to come up with a plan very quickly."

"Ain't nothin to plan. This is a forced marriage. I don't really know you. I don't love you, and I don't give a fuck about shit that has to do with Jamaica including you. I got some bidness to take care of in a few hours. You do what you do. I ain't got nothing to do with that."

Ashlynn looked hurt, she swallowed the lump in her throat and nodded her head. "Cool then. You gon' head and do you. I'll be okay. I always have been, and I always will be." She slipped into the bed and pulled the covers over her head. "Make sure you shower before you come back from her house. I hate the smell of a woman's filth. At least honor that."

I sucked my teeth. "Whatever, shorty, take yo monka ass to sleep. I'll see you when I get back."

"Whatever." She turned off the lamp that was on the side of the bed, and the basement went dark.

I felt bad for how I'd talked to her, but I also felt it was necessary. Ashlynn was a beautiful woman. If I allowed myself to fall under her physical spell, I was sure to be in trouble. I didn't want to feel anything for her. It was too dangerous. My heart screamed for Tasia and her dark-skin that was like the most beautiful sunset ever seen. I hated Jamaica, and therefore I disliked Ashlynn. She was a constant reminder of my imprisonment to my father, and my detesting of the island.

I grabbed my car keys after dressing and was ready to hit the road. I couldn't wait to see Tasia. When I got to the top of the steps King was waiting there shirtless with a machete in his hand. It spooked me so bad that I almost slipped down the stairs.

"Where are you going dis time of di night, Tyson?" His eyes were bloodshot red.

"I need some fresh air. I'm finna take a drive. Is that okay with you?" I tried to go up the stairs.

He placed the machete to my throat and leaned into my face. "Dis is not dee time to chase some bum gal. You have a wife to concentrate on. Go back down dare and be with her. Do it." The blade felt sharp against my throat as if at any moment it would slice into my flesh.

I swallowed my spit and flexed my muscles. My nostrils flared. I looked down on the blade, and then up into his bloodshot eyes. I could smell the Brandy and Ganja smoke all over him.

"Yeah, a'ight Pops, I'ma do just that."

"Good." He removed the blade from my neck and left from the top of the stairs closing the door to the basement's entrance behind him.

I sat on the steps and began to shake. I covered my face with my hands and forced myself to calm down. I needed to break the yoke that King had around me. I still didn't know how I was going to do it, or when, but it was nagging at me worse than ever now.

Chapter 10

Two weeks later King led me into one of the big buildings in downtown New York early in the morning. It was a bright and sunny day, with barely any wind. There were ten of his bodyguards following close behind us. The dress code was Tom Ford's three-piece suits, and even though I didn't have a lick of paperwork inside mine, King wanted me to carry a leather briefcase. We looked like a bunch of professional men headed to trade stocks in the stock market but knowing my father anything legit was the furthest thing from his mind.

When we got inside the building, we took the elevator to the twentieth floor. Each man was quiet inside. I could hear the elevator moving up the wire. My stomach churned when it came to a stop and a bell went off. The doors opened and we stepped out to the sight of a Spanish man buffing the floors with his earbuds in his ears, but it was so loud that I could hear the Mariachi music coming from his speakers. We walked past him, and I followed my father.

He led the pack as if he owned the big building, and I wouldn't have been surprised if he had at least a stake in it. When we got to the boardroom King turned around and looked specifically at me.

He placed his hand on my left shoulder. "Tyson, pay attention to dee men in da room and take everyting very seriously. You are da Prince of da Fast Muney Cartel. You must see what takes place in a room like dis. Okay, son?"

"Yeah, Pop, I got you." I didn't know if my father thought I was slow or what, but he sure had a way of making me feel like I was the way he looked me over as if he didn't think I understood what was going on.

"A'ight, let's go." He tapped on the doors with his big Black knuckles.

It took a moment for the doors to open. When they did there were two big, beefy, white men standing there looking out at us. They had earpieces in their ears as if they were Secret Servicemen. They back away from the wooden doors and allowed my father's entourage to come inside the room.

We walked into it. The room was huge, it looked as if it was made of oakwood all around. There were eight other men inside it and they were armed. My father's men took their places around the expanse of the room so that for each armed man that was standing around we had a man to watch him that was also armed. Our armed men had dreads that fell below their waists. Their eyes were red, and their skin was blacker than a shadow.

My Pops, King walked up to the front of the boardroom where the Mayor of New York was seated smoking on a cigar. He had two big bodyguards behind him. King extended his hand, and the mayor shook it.

"Nice tuh buck up again, Cuomo." King looked down at him.

Cuomo pulled out a chair that was on his right side. "Have a seat, Locust. I take it you've brought me a gift."

King placed his briefcase on the table and opened it for Cuomo. He pulled out two yellowish, orange colored pounds of Kingston Ganja. The scent was so loud that it filled the boardroom. He slid them in front if Cuomo and then placed another suitcase on the table that was filled with cash.

"One hunnit' thousand dolla' right dare', and sum' of dee' best smoke from dee' eye-lond' you could ever chief."

Cuomo puffed on his cigar. "Thank you." He bowed his head. "Now let's talk business."

King held up his hand. "Ma' didn't come to negotiate anyting mon', mi waan Harlem from St. Nicholas all di' way until da' borough ends. Ma' don't worry about the street wars that I'll have ta be involved in. Ma' take it as it comes. Di only worry is di feds. Dat's where you come in."

Cuomo was an Italian man in every sense of the word. His rosy-colored face, his thick brown hair with the gray streaks speckled through it, and his Italian nose. He was dressed sharply in a two-piece Italian suit.

"It's gonna take a lot more than a hundred thousand dollars and all of this good marijuana to get me to budge in any direction when it comes to Harlem. Besides, Kammron is home now. He's already put some things in place that sound financially beneficial for the entire city. Why would I step on his toes when he is one of the reasons that I am in this position that I am sitting in?"

King frowned his face. He lowered his eyelids and sat back in his chair. "Kammron is a joke. Ya' kint' possibly tink' dat he will keep his words. Kammron has always been a snake."

Cuomo shook his head. "Maybe to the men inside the Coke Kings but never too old Cuomo here. Because of Kammron I am Mayor of the city and set to be Governor very soon. You should already know that when it comes to New York everything is political. If you can help to advance a campaign, then you have worth. In this industry, if you aren't able to be used then you are useless. It's plain and simple."

"Before Kammron was released ya' told me dat' Harlem was for the Rastas. I got my men together' for dose purposes. A real man kin' neva' go back on his word. Ma' don't give a fuck 'bout dee Coke Kings. I will crush Kammron for Harlem. Ya' need to get out of dee' way and name yuh price." King pulled a blunt out of his suit pocket. His bodyguard sparked it for him.

"What's the drug of choice for Harlem?" Cuomo asked, breaking down a spare cigar, and taking the time to pinch off the Ganja my father had bought him. It surprised the hell out of me when he sat there and actually twisted up his blunt just like somebody from the hood. Then he lit it.

"We got it all. Harlem will always be for the horse, but we will introduce some of dee' crystal Meth amongst other tings'." King blew a cloud of smoke into the air.

Cuomo smiled. "And my cut?"

"Twenty-five percent a sale. Ya' cyaan' beat dat' price. Ma' still hafeta' pay off yer' police force dat walk da' certain beats. Not to mention all dee' other costs." King dumped the ashes from his blunt and took two more pulls from it.

"Thirty percent a sale, and I will introduce you to this new drug called Krokadil. It's taking over the drug market in Russia and the kingpins out there are getting filthy rich because of it. New York needs to explore it. You already know that whenever a new drug hits our test markets or the inner city. When it comes to New York we flood Harlem first. Your systems in the Black community are the strongest followed by the Latinos. Once we are able to determine what this drug does to you guys, and the long-term effects of its usage only then will we feel free enough to sample it in white America." Cuomo puffed his weed and seemed to look and see what effects his words would have on my father.

King appeared to brush it off. "Ma" heard 'bout dis' ear' Krokadil. Let's try it. If mi effect the epicenter of Black pee'ple yuh percentage is twenty percent all around di board, not counting di personal donations of bodies yuh need tuh disappear within unnu owna community."

Cuomo rubbed the sparse hairs on his chin. "And the war between you and Kammron will not affect my twenty percent no matter how out of hand it gets?"

King shook his head. "Di Coke Kings are mi business. Yuh money a yours an dat a ih.."

Cuomo was lost in thought for a moment. He slowly began to shake his head. "We get shipments of the Krokadil in America in two weeks. Atlanta, Washington D.C., Detroit, South Carolina as a whole, Los Angeles, and Harlem, New York will be the dumping posts. You will be in charge of the Krokadil here. Show me that you know how to infect those people down there and Harlem, along with Brooklyn is yours. You will have my protection from law enforcement. Deal?" Cuomo extended his hand.

King stood up from the table and extended his hand. "Deal."

***

That night I laid on my back in the bed trying to make some sense of the things that I had heard my father talking about with the mayor of New York. It seemed to me that King wasn't doing anything other than selling the health of our people to the mayor for his own selfish reasons. I didn't know that this was how things were handled behind the scenes. But I always wondered how others were able to sell dope for a short period of time before they were caught where others were able to sell it for thirty years without so much as a citation.

Now I understood that those in power actually used our own people within the community to infect us, and their rewards for doing so was the money, games, and fortune, along with the avoidance of prison as long as they played by Uncle Sam's rules. The Trap was more complicated than I'd ever really imagined.

Ashlynn turned on her side to face me. She saw that I was up and placed her hand on my chest. "Tyson, what's the matter?" She rubbed her hand from side to side. It felt good.

"I'm just up thinking right now. I got a lot on my mind and it's making me restless."

She crawled over until her head was on my chest. Over the past few weeks, she and I had begun to grow a bit closer together. King was basically forcing us to be under each other all the time. She was kind of growing on me.

"Is there anything I can do to make you feel better?" She trailed her hand over my stomach and kept going down until she was cuffing my piece through my boxers. My dick spring right up.

"I'm saying, do you think that you're ready to go there with me?" I felt my piece jumping up and down as if it couldn't contain itself.

She rolled onto her stomach and sat back on her haunches. Her short nightgown moved up her thick thighs. There was enough light in the room for me to be able to see her pink panties. The sight was arousing because I felt like I was peeking at her and she didn't know it.

"Baby, sooner or later we're going to have to coexist. To be honest, I like you. You're not a total asshole like the other men in Jamaica. It's nice to see that the Jamaican side of you didn't turn you into a jerk." She pulled my piece through the boxer hole and stroked me. "So, what do you say?"

I was laid back with my stomach muscles popping. "I'm ready for you, too."

Tasia crossed my mind. I had to block her out for now. We hadn't spoken in a week. She was mad at me and thought that I was intentionally blowing her off for Ashlynn when in actuality King was making it nearly impossible for us to have any contact. He was on my ass like a pair of underwear.

Ashlynn licked her juicy lips. "Okay, den'." She kissed the head and rested her lips on the top of it. Her tongue traced circles all around it before she sucked just the tip into her mouth five quick times. She popped it out and proceeded to pump me up and down. "Do you know every time you go to sleep on your back that this big thing finds its way out of your boxer hole and sticks straight up. One time I even did something I'm embarrassed to say to myself while I stared at it for thirty minutes. This is a lot." She sucked it back into her mouth and closed her eyes while she performed.

I moaned and groaned. She opened her eyes and her hazel eyes beamed into mine. She smiled and went to work. I shuddered when she purposely grazed her teeth over the soft skin before she sucked me halfway down. She gagged and came back up. Her small fist beat it some more.

"I wanna fuck, Ashlynn. You got me so mafuckin' horny right now. I need to see what that pussy feels like." I reached under her gown and rubbed the front of her panties pushing the material into her hot, soft, moist lips. "You gon' let me hit this pussy?" I yanked the material to the side exposing her hairy golden box.

"Mmm, yeah. Come on." She rolled onto her back and pulled her gown back.

The panties were already stuck to the right side of her sex lips. She rubbed her middle finger through them and opened her folds so I could see her pink.

I was shaking, I got into a push-up position and climbed in between her gap. My nose went right into her center. I inhaled and swiped my tongue upward. She moaned and placed her bare feet on the bed cocking them wide open. Two of my fingers spread her lips wider. Her clitoris popped out. It was erect and glossy. "You smell good girl." I sniffed her some more.

"Unnhhh, what?" Her small hands went up and pulled her breasts out of her gown.

"You heard me." I kissed her lips and sucked on one at a time while she dug her nails into my shoulder blades arching her back and moaning loudly.

I pulled her down by her hips and pressed her knees to her chest making her bust that kitty wide open. I sniffed it again. Her scent was intoxicating. I think I was just obsessed with the natural scent of a woman period, but either way, she was driving me crazy. My tongue attacked her clitoris at full speed, then I was sucking on it like a nipple.

She bucked into my face. "Uhhh! Uhhh! Tyson!" She came throwing her ankles around my shoulders and forcing my head further into her sex. She mashed it around until she came again. "I'm ready. I'm ready. Please fuck me, Tyson."

I was between her thighs fast. I rubbed her pussy for a full minute, pinching the lips together until she was so wet that her juices were oozing out of her. I rubbed my dick up and down her entrance and slid into her hot oven like a knife into room temperature butter. She gasped with her mouth wide open. My eyes rolled into the back of my head. I pulled her closer to me and placed her left ankle on my right shoulder. I slammed into her.

"Uh, shit. Shit, baby. That's deep, wait a minute." She tried to sit up.

My hips pulled back. I slammed into her again. Then I was long stroking that Jamaican pussy like an animal on a mission. She felt tight and hot. Her juices dripped off my balls every time I pounded into her. The feeling kept getting better and better. I felt like a damn fool having let her spend so many nights in my bed without tapping that ass.

She climbed up and bit into my neck. She sucked and licked all over the left side of my face. This made me fuck her with all my might while I growled like an angry lion. She threw her right thigh around my waist and screamed cumming hard.

I pushed both of her knees to her chest and fucked her at full speed until I came deep inside of her channel. "Uh! Uh! Fuck! Shit!" My hips popped forward milking myself. I fell on top of her.

She rolled us over until she was on top. She leaned down and kissed my lips. "You're amazing, Tyson. Fuck, that was so good." More kisses ensued.

I rubbed all over her ass and tried to catch my breath. Sweat ran down my forehead. I could smell the scent of us. I closed my eyes once an image of Tasia came across my mind. I felt like I'd betrayed her.

Ashlynn curled up to me and hugged my body. "As much as I hated to admit it. I'm starting to like America. I miss Odana but we Facetimed and she is okay. For now, you are my focus. I'm growing into you." She closed her eyes and left me awake in deep thought.

Chapter 11

The next few months were spent with King getting everything in order. He brought over so many soldiers from Jamaica that soon Red Hook was looking like the island. Niggas were running around with long dreads hollering that they were King crazy. That they ran under my father and would die for him in a heartbeat. When they saw me, they bowed their heads as his young Prince even though I had yet to pick up a sack. I appreciated the respect and admiration but no matter where I went, I always felt like I was being watched, or trailed. I didn't like the feeling of incarceration. I thought about breaking free every single day.

Four months into us coming back from Jamaica Tasia had me blocked on all her social media sites and she had her phone number changed. I was sick over this. I thought about her every other minute and wondered how and what she was doing. From the meetings I knew first-hand, King was waiting to go to war with Kammron and the Coke Kings. I didn't know when, or how the war was going to jump off, but I knew it was a sure thing.

King was already moving troops toward Harlem and all-over upper Manhattan. Some of the young killas that he moved in looked as if they didn't care about nothing but murder. They wore all-black and kept half of their faces covered with Jamaican colored masks. They were strapped as if it were Armageddon. I kept my distance because I only got bad murderous vibes from being around them.

Halfway through the first month, King encouraged me to take Ashlynn out for a date night. He must've been tired of us being cooped up in the house all the time. I didn't mind it, I didn't see any reason to be out and about with so much preparation for war and tension brewing between The Fast

Money Cartel and the Coke Kings, though Kammron and his crew had yet to show any signs of aggression toward the Rastas led by my father. I didn't know if Kammron was going to willingly give up Harlem or if he was going to fight for it, but I guess we did the latter. Just like my father was a living legend in Kingston, Jamaica. Kammron was a legend in New York, especially uptown in the borough of Harlem so I expected a lot of bloodshed when the war finally kicked off.

On the night I was set to take Ashlynn out, I got dressed from head to toe in a black and red Chanel outfit with the Balenciaga shoes to match. My neck was flooded with a few good chains, and I had two diamonds in each one of my ears. My pants were a bit snug but I was fresh. My hair was newly edged up, and I had the top nappy but neat. I smelled like a million bucks and felt even better.

Ashlynn wanted to match my fly and she did just that. When she stepped out of the bathroom in a black and red double C skirt dress that was so tight I could see her nipples through the fabric. Her ass was poked out like a stomach, and her make-up was on point. Her curly hair fell all over her shoulders, and this night her eyes seemed greener than hazel.

She sprayed some perfume on her neck and walked toward me. "How do I look?" She made her eyeliner look like she was Asian around the eyes.

"Yo' damn how you look for a minute. I was out of the bathroom first. Tell a nigga how he looking and smelling?" I turned in a small circle so she could peep my duggy.

She placed her hand on her right hip. "Really, babe, you gotta go first?"

"I spent just as much time putting this shit together as you did. Now how is a mafucka looking?"

She snickered. "You're fresh, baby. My husband is fine as wine before you pop the cork." She walked up to me and ran her hand over my shirt. "I mean that."

"Aw I know. I saw me before you did." I stepped away from her and grabbed my car keys.

She crossed her arms. "Okay, what about me?"

"What about you, what?" I dusted myself off and checked my lining in the mirror that was on top of my dresser.

"How do I look?" She held her arms out at her sides.

I knew what she was talking about, and I knew what she was expecting to hear but I couldn't give that to her. You see Ashlynn was so fine that she was used to niggas all over her ass and giving her compliment after compliment. If I fell into the same category with other niggas, then she would look at me just like she did them. I needed to step outside of that box. I was my own man.

"Well?" She held her arms out and turned in a circle.

I kept looking in the mirror at myself. "That's the outfit that I bought for you?"

"Yeah, don't it look good on me?"

"It looks straight, but I think I shoulda got you the other one. This doesn't look all that good on you." I turned to face her. "I think you might've put on too much make-up."

She touched her face. "I thought it was perfect."

I shrugged my shoulders. "It doesn't matter Che' Henri gon' be dark anyway. Come on let's rollout."

"Damn." She stepped in front of the mirror looking somber. She touched her face and turned her head sideways. She made a circle in the mirror and sighed. "I tried." She grabbed her jacket and sunk her shoulders as she walked past me.

I smiled behind her back and shook my head. She was looking so fine that I felt a bit intimidated. But I bounced back like a basketball real quick from that feeling. After all, I was a Prince.

***

"I still can't believe that you ain't never had a triple cheese lasagna before. What the fuck they be feeding y'all in Jamaica?" I poured myself some of the Moët that was on the table. Che' Henri was a nice French restaurant located right off Times Square. It had mood lighting and Maître Dees that were dressed in black and white that paid special attention specifically to our table. The music coming through the speakers was in French, but it still was soothing.

Ashlynn pushed her plate away from her. She had only nibbled from her lasagna. She crossed her arms around her body like she had a habit of doing and sat back. "We eat good food there, but I just don't have an appetite right now." The lights from the candles flickered in her eyes.

"What's the matter, Ashlynn?"

"Nothing?"

"Man, what's the matter? You were hungry at first when I told you about this restaurant. So, now what's wrong with you?"

"Nothing."

"Yo' tell me what's good man?" I flared my nostrils at her.

She slammed her small hand on the table. "I took three hours getting ready for yo' monka ass, and you gon' tell me that I look okay? Boy, you done fucked my night all up. Legit." She frowned and rolled her eyes, giving me the stank face. I guess they did that in Jamaica, too.

"Yo' that's why you're acting all funny and shit?" I picked up my champagne and drank some of it. It tickled my throat going down.

100

"You damn right. You crushed my self-esteem. I know you don't like light-skinned females and all that but I am your wife now. You need to see me for who I am physically and love me. Damn." She looked down at her lap and remained quiet.

I set down the glass. "Ashlynn?"

She refused to look at me. "What?"

"Are you really starting to feel me like that, though?"

"Shid, I was but now you got me feeling like I ain't good enough. I don't know how to feel about you." She exhaled and fanned her eyes while she kept them wide open. "I've been trying so hard, Tyson. I know this relationship is forced, and we would never have been together, but I am trying. I'm only eighteen years old. What more do you want from me?"

I slid around the booth and wrapped my arm around her shoulder. "Hand to God, Ashlynn. You look good as a muthafucka. You are crushing shit baby and I apologize for not telling you that sooner." I kissed her cheek.

"You mean that?" She started to perk up.

"Yeah, I mean that. I wanted to tell you how bad you look but I already know you are used to hearing that shit from every nigga you come in contact with. I ain't trying to be kissing yo' ass like them."

She looked at me. "It's not even like that. My whole life men have done nothing but take advantage of me. They treated me like a sex doll and made me feel like I was nothing more than a piece of meat. I was never complimented or told that I was good enough. Beautiful never came out of their mouths." She sighed. "Tyson, since I have been here in America your family has treated me better than I have ever been treated in all my life. I appreciate all of you. I know that you are the key to this treatment, so I am willing to submit to you. All I ask is that you love and respect me. After all, I am nothin' more than a delicate flower in need of your watering. I wanna love you. Please let me grow to do so." She hugged my side.

I held her. "I will. We're just kids, we'll figure this thing out."

"Your father told me I had three more months to come up pregnant or he was getting rid of me in a way that I would never forget. I don't know what that means but it is terrifying." She shivered against me.

"How can you say that this is the best that you have ever been treated if he is saying things like this to you?"

"Because my life has been nothing but abuse and pain. His words are only words? Actions are what I have experienced. Sometimes I welcome death but then I think about Odana. She needs me."

"I need you, too." I kissed her forehead. "I guess I gotta start beating them guts up, huh?"

She snickered. "I guess so. You be doing your thang anyway. I can admit that."

I slipped my hand under her skirt and rubbed her pussy through the panties. "When you're built like this and you got a husband like me, I am supposed to be all over you all the time. I gotta get better emotionally for you but I will get there. I promise I will." I guided her face until she was lip to lip with me. We kissed.

I licked all over her suckable lips and kissed her hard. Our tongues played over one another's. My fingers were in her panties. They slipped inside of her hairy sex and went deep. She moaned.

Slam!

I jumped back ready to grab the gun that was in my lower back. When I looked up, I saw Tasia dressed in a waitress's outfit looking down on me with a frown on her face. She looked from me then over at Ashlynn, and back to me again. She shook her head and walked away.

I got ready to climb away from the table to go after her when Ashlynn pulled me back. She wrapped her arm around my neck and mugged Tasia's back. Her hand went into my lap. "I'm yo' mafuckin' wife, screw her. Matter of fact, let's get out of here."

I sat there for a minute stuck. I wanted to go and find out what Tasia was doing working there? When had she gotten the job? What was going on in her life? How much had she seen transpire between me and Ashlynn?

Ashlynn tried to pull me up, I didn't move. She winced and looked over to Tasia. Tasia was cleaning a table and mumbling to herself. Ashlynn looked back to me. "What, you wanna go over there and say somethin' to her don't you?"

I nodded. "Yeah, we fell off on such crazy terms. I just need to let her know what's good."

Ashlynn frowned her face. "You don't owe anybody any explanations. She is a problem. I am your wife and if we were in Jamaica right now, I would be forced to kill her over you." Her eyes were bright green now. She tilted her head forward and lowered her eyes.

I sat there watching Tasia. Finally, I stood up. "Calm yo' lil' yellow ass down. I just need to holler at her for one minute." I left our table with Ashlynn waving me off. When I got to Tasia she rolled her eyes and proceeded to pick up the dirty plates from one of the tables that she was bussing down. "I thought that was a bus boy's job?"

"We're understaffed right now. What do you want?" She gathered the dishes and headed to the back of the restaurant with me following behind her. She stopped mid-stride and frowned at me. "I ain't fuckin' wit' you no more, Tyson. Take yo' married ass over there with her. I wish both of you the best."

Ashlynn appeared beside me. She slid her arm around my lower waist. "Look, girl, I don't know who you are, but this is my husband. You need to go and find your own. I ain't playin' about him."

Tasia set the dishes on a table that was close to her. "Bitch, who are you talking to? You got me fucked up. This is Brooklyn, right here."

Ashlynn began to remove her earrings. "I don't care where you from. I'll fuck you up about mine." She dropped her earrings into her skirt dress pocket. "Fuck you wanna do?"

A heavy-set French man came out of the back with a worried expression on his face. He had been watching us for a time. "Excuse me but is there a problem?"

"This waitress is an excellent employee. Thank you again for the help ma'am." I placed my arm around Ashlynn and walked her out of the restaurant after placing two hundred dollars into the bill folder that was on our table. We drove home in silence.

Chapter 12

Maze woke me up at five in the morning three weeks later with his face balled into a mask of anger. "Say, Kid, I need you to roll out wit' me to Harlem. I just got robbed and I ain't about to take that shit lying down." He started to pace back and forth in the basement. My Pops was out of town, and my mother Angela had always looked at Maze like her son. That was the only reason he was in my basement.

Ashlynn pulled the covers firmer over her body. "I don't know who that bombaclat is but tell him to be quiet Honey. My head is pounding."

Maze kneeled and picked up her pink thongs with his index finger. He held it up and smiled. "I ain't seen how Shorty look outside of that bed but from here she looks thick as a mafucka. She can watch her mouth with all that bombaclat shit, though. I got some Rastafarian homies and they say that shit mean Bitch ass nigga. Word to Brooklyn ain't no ho in da god." He sniffed the crotch of her panties.

I yanked them bitches out of his hand and mugged his nasty ass. "Kid, that's my wife. Fuck is you doing?" I was ready to knock his black ass clean out wit' his perverted ass."

"My bad dawg, you know how shit be when you got them Percocets in you." He scratched his arm. "You fuckin' wit' me or not?"

Twenty minutes later I was leaving the house and jumping into his black Navigator. I leaned the seat back. Before we pulled off Maze pulled out a small saucer and snorted two lines of Mollie off it. He pulled his nose and tried to pass the saucer to me. I pushed that shit back to him. I didn't fuck wit' Mollie. I didn't like how that shit made him act and I feared what it would do to my system.

When Maze finished, he pulled away from the curb. He turned up a rap group called Griselda. They were from Brooklyn where we're from and to me, they had the streets of New York.

"Yo', it's been so long since I was caught slipping that I don't know how to take this shit in." He pulled his nose and sniffed hard.

"What the fuck happened anyway?"

"We were over on a hundred and fortieth and St. Nicholas shooting dice. I was running up a check and you already know how I get when I get up on a nigga. I got to talking that Brooklyn is the best borough shit, and niggas got mad. I ain't give a fuck about they feelings. I got up to forty-eight hunnit and was ready to smash out. But before I could come off one knee one of them bitch ass Harlem niggas put that Blicka to my neck."

In New York, another word for pistol is Blicka, especially in the slums of Brooklyn.

"Yo' what you do when that nigga put that heat to you, Kid?"

"I let him go in my pockets and take what he wanted. He hit me for nine thousand and some odd cents. I want every penny of my shit back. What's fucked up is that I know who da lil' fuck nigga is. Some niggas are okay with committing suicide I guess." He kept cruising. He looked over at me with glossy eyes. "Yo' that pink whore is blazing. You need to see what it do wit' Shorty." He was talking about the pink Mollie.

"I'm good, Kid. The God don't need any habits. I gotta stay focused."

Maze smacked his lips and sucked his teeth. "Fa what, Dunn, yo Pops doing every fuckin' thing. You might not ever have to touch the slums in yo' life if you don't want to. You got an easy ass ride. King Locust is the man."

I mugged him. "I don't need nobody taking care of me. You talking 'bout my old man like he saving me or something. You ain't the only mafucka that'll get down in these streets. Fuck you talking 'bout?"

Maze pursed his lips, then started laughing. "Nigga if you don't shut yo' lil' soft ass up. Fuck you got like one body under yo' belt? That goofy from Jamaica. Nigga please." He cracked up laughing again.

"I don't see shit funny. What, you think you hard 'cause you got a few under yours or something?"

"Not a few, twenty. I done murked twenty mafuckas and if I find this nigga slipping tonight it's gon' be twenty-one with no mercy." He sniffed and pulled on his nose for a moment. "I love killing. That shit is in my soul. If he wouldn't have gotten the ups on me, I would have smoked him and every nigga that was at the gamble like it wasn't nothing. But it's all good, though. That bitch ass nigga gotta answer for his sins like he speaking to Lucifer himself." He nodded his head hard to the Griselda track.

"You sure you know where this fool stays?" Maze was high as a kite and I was starting to have second thoughts about fuckin' wit' him.

I didn't care how many murders I had under my belt. I wasn't dead set on catching anymore that night, but I would have my homie's back like I was supposed to. I was a Brooklyn nigga, and in Brooklyn, we expressed loyalty by shedding blood for those that we loved. I loved Maze more than my own father. In fact, he was the only male that I cared about because we had been holding each other down since we were shorties.

"Yeah, I know where his bitch ass stay. I fuck wit' one of the nigga's baby mothers. She wants his trifling ass out the way, and I am going to respectfully slump his bitch ass. Then

I'ma go and knock her shit loose. Or did I already do it?" He covered his mouth with his hand. "I guess we finna find out."

I shook my head. "Whatever nigga, let's just go and get this shit over wit', word up."

***

I crept beside the masked Maze as he stood under the open bedroom window. It was scorching hot outside. My face was itching under my black ski mask. Mosquitoes were flying around and biting as if they were starving. I'd smacked more than one before I squat down with the .45 in my hand. I was shaking. I wasn't afraid, I was ready to go up into this apartment and handle business. There was a full moon in the sky.

Maze leaned into my ear. "That bitch told me that this window would be open right here. She said it was stuck open. She called his bitch ass a few minutes ago and he told her he was at home. He ain't got no whip wit' his bum ass." Maze looked both ways while he squatted on the side of the gangway. He wiped the sweat from his forehead. "Yo' give me a boost, Kid." He lifted his right LeBron.

I clasped my fingers and allowed him to step into them. When he did, I lifted him up and he climbed into the window. He turned around and looked down at me. "Go to the back door. I'll be there in a second." He cocked his .40 Glock and disappeared inside of the window.

I jogged to the back of the house and ducked down. Sweat was pouring down my back. Now that he was inside the house I was nervous. I knew for a fact we were about to have to kill some shit and that terrified me. I felt stupid I was wishing I had never gotten into that truck now, but it was too late.

King of the Trap

Maze opened the back door slowly with his finger to his lips. He waved me inside. I smelled the scent of marijuana mixed with cocaine right away. In New York, we called this a Primo. Usually, the weed smokers that were about to transition to crack cocaine smoked their joints or blunts like this. Maze headed up the back steps. He stopped suddenly and leaned into me.

"Dat bitch ass nigga here. His pants are in the living room. Look at this." He held up a wad of hundreds. "This is all my money right here. I still gotta have his ass, though." He crept up the steps.

When we got inside the apartment we stepped into the kitchen. It had Pizza Hut boxes all over the table. Maze zipped past me and into the hallway. He stopped outside the bedroom door that was located in the middle of the hallway. He placed his ear to it. He waved me over pointing to the door.

I came over and pointed my gun at the door ready for him to open it. Maze placed his hand around the knob. I cocked my position ready to blow at whatever was on the other side. Maze nodded at me and opened the door. As soon as he opened the bedroom door he rushed inside hollering. As he was doing this, I got the shock of my life when Tasia came out of the bathroom dressed in a pair of pink boy shorts, and a white beater that put her thick areolas on display. She screamed and threw her hands up for a moment before turning around and running toward the front door.

Smack! Smack! Smack! Smack!

"Bitch ass nigga; you thought it was sweet to steal from me?" More smacking ensued.

I heard hollering, then whimpering. Maze was cursing out his victim while he beat him senseless.

I caught Tasia at the door and slung her to the ground. The front room was dark except for the small television that was playing. "Get yo' ass down."

"No!" She jumped up and rushed me with her head down swinging wildly.

She punched me three hard times before I stuck out my leg and slung her backward. She landed hard on her back and grimaced. She laid there for a minute and tried to get up again. *Boom! Boom!* There was a slight pause. *Boom!*

Maze came out of the room with his gun smoking. He stepped into the living room with his eyes wide inside the mask. He stepped over Tasia and aimed his gun down at her. "Fuck dis bitch."

"Wait!" I jumped on top of her and covered her body with my own. I could feel her nails digging into my sides.

"Fuck is you doing, nigga?"

I pulled my mask off. "Nigga dis, my bitch. You ain't finna blow her."

Maze looked down for a clear shot. "Stop playing and move nigga."

"Tyson, that's you? Please don't let him kill me." She was shaking uncontrollably.

"I ain't, just calm down. Maze, this is Tasia, nigga."

Maze flipped on the light switch. He looked down at her and bucked his eyes. "Damn, bitch, what the fuck is you doing in here?"

"I-I-I work for Halstead at his strip club. Greg ordered me and the other dancer that was in the room with him to come over and dance for him. I just got undressed. Why are y'all here?"

"Damn, man." Maze tucked his pistol. "Man, I can't leave this bitch alive nigga. I ain't going back to jail for nobody.

Fuck that, move Tyson." He pulled his gun back out and aimed it at me.

"Never; I love dis girl man. I ain't finna let you kill her. I'll take the wrap for this shit if it ever comes out. But I already know that ain't no snitch in this Queen. You gotta let her pass on the strength of me."

Maze wavered with his finger on the trigger. "Man!" He shook and cursed. "This shit is on you, nigga. You already know how we get down in Brooklyn. This bitch is supposed to be dead like those other two in there. On the strength of you though, Tyson. Only for you, my nigga. I'm gone! Come on, she's coming, too!" He took off towards the back door.

I got up and pulled Tasia to her feet. "We need to wipe down these door handles and anything you touched before we get out of here. You can never talk about this day ever again. You know that don't you?"

She nodded. "You saved my life, Tyson. You saved my life and I swear to God I will repay you for this. I owe you my life." She hugged me hard for a long time, then kissed my lips. She sucked on them and rubbed my chest. "I'm sorry. N'all, fuck that, no I'm not."

I laughed briefly and pushed her toward the hallway. Grab yo' clothes. We gotta get out of here." She did just that and then we bounced from the house by use of the backdoor.

I kept feeling her lips upon mine. I kept smelling the scent of her perfume the entire time within my nostrils. From that one kiss, Tasia reentered my system and I couldn't get her off of my mind for the next few weeks.

T.J. Edwards

Chapter 13

It was a month after the lick in which Maze had smoked two people. Tasia and I had been in constant communication with each other. Though it was only reduced to FaceTiming and social media messages, we did it a lot. King was still on my ass and making sure Ashlynn and I were on top of her getting pregnant, and that both of us were spending as much time together alone as we could. I still didn't understand why it was so important that Ashlynn got pregnant but then again it was hard to figure King out sometimes.

It was October twentieth the day of Ashlynn's birthday when she woke me up with a blow horn in her mouth. She blew it as hard as she could and ran around the room blowing the horn over and over again. "It's my birthday! It's my birthday! It's my birthday! And guess what? We're pregnant!" She pulled two pregnancy tests out of her robe pocket and held them up for me as I stretched my arms.

I was just waking up. It took me a second to get my vision in order. Ashlynn came over and dropped the tests in my lap. I picked them up just as Hermés came into the room wearing a pair of sunglasses. She came over to me and hugged my body. She kissed my lips, and then wiped her kiss away with her thumb. I smiled and groggily looked over the tests.

"Read them and leap with joy. I got yo' baby inside me right now. I'm so happy, Tyson. And it's my birthday!" She blew the horn hard with her head tilted back.

My mother Angela came down the stairs with her fingers inside her ears. King was right behind her. His long gray and black dreadlocks swung at his waist.

My mother walked up to Ashlynn and snatched the horn out of her mouth. She mugged her and threw the horn to the floor.

Ashlynn backed up. "Why did you do that?" Her bottom lip quivered.

My mother lowered her eyes. "It is five o'clock in the got damn morning on a Sunday and you're blowing a damn horn. Knock it off. Everybody knows that it is your birthday. We get it."

"But it's not just my birthday, I'm pregnant. I'm going to be giving you your first grandchild." Ashlynn held her stomach. Her robe was a silk number, short and seductive. She stood there with her stomach poked out purposely. If not for her dramatics it would be hard to tell that she was even pregnant.

King moved my mother out of the way. He walked up to Ashlynn and placed his big, black hands on her stomach. His eyes were opened wide. He looked from Ashlynn then over to me. "Are you sure?"

She nodded. "Yep, both sticks came back positive. I have already made an appointment with my gynecologist for Thursday. I'm so happy, and it's my—"

Angela placed her finger on Ashlynn's lips. "If you say it's your birthday one more time this will be your last one. Now shut up and go to seep. Life is too precious to be dealing with such a loud girl." She waved her off and headed up the stairs.

Ashlynn watched Angela until she disappeared. She closed her eyes and tears came down her cheeks. "She doesn't like me. I don't know what I have done to her, but she just doesn't like me." She covered her face with her hands.

King pulled her to him and kissed her forehead. "Yer' are Jamaican. Don't worree' bout' Angela. Nobody iz' good enough fer' Tyson." He shook his head and held her tighter to him. "Princess, I'll have dee best birtday surprise fi yuh yet. Mi promise yuh dis'." He kissed her forehead again and smiled. Then he left the basement without looking back over his shoulder.

In all the years that I have known my Father, I had never seen him be more affectionate. This spooked me. It seemed like he was thirsty for me and Ashlynn to have this kid.

Ashlynn slid next to me and laid her head on my chest. "Baby, you haven't said anything. Aren't you happy that we are finally going to have a baby?" She was in my face now.

"Yeah, lil' bruh ain't you happy?" Hermés stood beside Ashlynn with a smile on her face.

I was still holding the tests in my hands. I was in disbelief. *A kid? Right now?* Hell, I felt like I was still a kid myself. I didn't think I was ready for this sort of responsibility. "Baby, I'm happy, of course, I am. This is what you wanted, right?"

She nodded. "Well, I didn't at first but slowly but surely just being around you and your family convinced me that this is where I am supposed to be, and so does our child. I am so happy. I mean I am sick over Angela hating my guts but other than that I am thankful that I will be able to enjoy this experience with you. I really care about you, Tyson." She hugged me.

It took me a second to hug her back. There was no way that she could care about me in the capacity that she was saying. I hadn't done anything for her that was worthy of such care. I was guessing that maybe being pregnant had her emotions all over the place. Either way, I was confused.

Hermés and I locked eyes. She gave me a weird look before she walked away shaking her head. "Tyson, come holler at me when you get a chance. We need to talk." She smiled looking over her shoulder at us. "Congratulations, you two. That's pretty awesome."

Neither Ashlynn nor I said a word. We waited for a full two minutes after Hermés was gone before we even moved in the slightest.

Then she slipped from my embrace. She ran her fingers through her hair and paced in front of the couch for a time before and she sat down and crossed her legs. "I'm lying Tyson."

"What?" I didn't think I'd heard her correctly. "Say that again."

"I said that I am lying. I'm not pregnant but your father said that if I wasn't pregnant soon, he would dispose of me and I believe him." She lowered her head and began to rub her temples in a circular motion. "What the fuck am I going to do when he finds out that I am not?"

My head was screwed up. "Wait a minute, how did you get those tests to say that you are then?"

"I have my ways and it doesn't matter. The bottom line is that I'm not. So, either we have to get cracking fast here, or King is going to kill me. I am sure of that. You aren't going to tell him, are you?"

"N'all." I came and sat next to her. "What the fuck are we doing, Ashlynn? How are we allowing this one man to run and ruin our lives the way that he is?"

She shrugged her shoulders. "I don't know but that seems to be what we're doing. It's either follow his rules or lose our lives. I don't know how severe the consequences can get for you, but for me and Odana, it is death. That is a pill that is too big to swallow."

I rubbed her back. "We gon' figure shit out. All we gotta do is get logical and find a way to break away from him. Do you think we can do that?"

"How can you and I do anything together when you don't even love me? Your heart is with another woman. You don't look at me the way that you do her and it crushes me every time I think about it. I know that I can be an amazing woman to you if you simply give me the chance to be."

"That's just the thing though, Ashlynn. You're already good enough. If I don't see that as a man, then that is my loss. A woman should never have to jump through hoops in order for a man to love her. It should happen naturally. I can feel in my heart that you are a blessing of a woman. Don't think anything less than that, please."

She turned toward me. "Then why won't you give me a real chance? What does Tasia have that I lack except her skin color?" She rested her hand on my shoulder. "Please tell me, I need to know."

I didn't have the right words when it came to her questions. I wish I did. All I could speak was the truth and how I really felt. "Tasia is from New York like me. We grew up around each other. I always found her beautiful, plus we got this unspoken bond that nobody will ever understand. I care about her, but I also care about you. I'm young, I don't know much about the settling down shit or how I am supposed to feel before I do it. All I can say now is that my heart is being pulled into two different directions. I got love for you, Ashlynn. I connect with your pain, and the lost soul inside of you."

"I have never needed anybody to blow smoke up my ass. I'm a big girl. Always have been, and I always will be. To be honest with you, Tyson. You don't have a choice to love outside of me. I am your wife. I am supposed to be number one on your list no matter what you feel toward anybody else. You suppress that shit." She leaned further into my face. "Love me like I am supposed to be loved. Love me like I deserve or allow your father to kill me. I need you, and I wanna be with you. Grant me those same feelings or pick out my tombstone." She got up and walked toward the stairs. "I don't care how premature it may seem to you, but I love you, Tyson." She sighed, turned, and went up the stairs leaving me warring with my own mind.

I really did like Ashlynn. I honestly felt that she could turn out to be an incredible wife if I gave her the chance to do so. But our lives were so forced and controlled. Every time I looked at her with enamor or emotion I didn't know if I was actually feeling those things or if I was being forced to feel them by King's mental manipulations. Either way, I had to figure out quickly what we were going to do.

***

That night my mother called me into her room. King was gone, and she was fresh from the shower. When I walked into her room, she ordered me to close the door and handed me a bottle of lotion. She sat on the bed and turned away from me. She pulled her robe down to expose her back to me. "You know I don't like that girl, right?"

I squirted the lotion into my hand. Like the rest of our family, my mother suffered from a slight case of eczema. From time to time either myself or Hermes would rub lotion onto her back for her because it was a hard place to reach.

"Yeah, I can tell. Why do you think that is, though?" I squirted just a bit more lotion into my hand before applying it to her back in a circular motion.

She groaned and leaned forward. "That feels good." She was quiet for a second while I rubbed. "I don't trust her son. Something about her just makes me feel like she is up to evil. I can feel it deep within my spirit. Plus, your father is too fond of her. Did you know that there is a bloody war going on in Kingston because of both Ashlynn and Manifest?

King of the Trap

Nobody understands or knows the importance of Ashlynn other than your father. I am hired easily with the Jamaican culture. All I know is that Ashlynn carries Marley blood inside of her. Marley blood is Royal blood when it comes to Jamaica. If you are to have a child with her that would make your father a part of the Royal bloodline. He could be the rightful king of the island and all the other places that Jamaica controls, which is a lot. I don't understand why he craves power so badly. Mmm, that feels so good." She crawled across the bed and laid on her stomach. She pulled the robe down to her lower waist. I straddled a knee on each side of her and kept rubbing her down. She laid with her face on her hands making noises deep within her throat. Her eyes were closed. "Honey, can you give me a quick massage? It's been so long, and my back is killing me."

"I got you ma'."

She took the robe completely off, and dropped it on the floor of her bedroom? She lay there in just her panties. "Another thing I don't like about her is that she and your father are always spending time alone whispering as if they are up to something. He is my husband. There shouldn't be any woman that knows more about what's going on with him than me."

I massaged her back and rubbed down to her lower waist. I applied pressure there because I knew she liked that. My mother had always gotten extremely bad lower back pains when it was time for her period. I made sure that I laid great detail to all of her problem areas around her waist. Then I moved upward. She arched her back and pushed back into me.

"So, what do you think I should do when it comes to Ashlynn? Should we have this baby?" I worked her slider blades, and down her spine.

"She's not pregnant. Any idiot can tell that those pregnancy sticks are doctored. Your father is so naive. The doctor will prove that she isn't really pregnant, and he will kill her. At least that is what he says but you never know. He treats her more like a daughter than he does Hermés. Lower baby."

I traveled lower and applied pressure on her lower back again. I dug into it with my fingers and pushed down on it over and over. She whimpered for a moment and then began to shake. I kept the pressure steady for a moment, then rubbed up her back. I kissed her cheek and pulled her robe back up. She turned on her side and tied the sash. Then she pulled me behind her.

I scooted to her back and held her. "When is King getting back home?"

"He left for Jamaica. He'll be there for a few days and then he will return home. I don't wanna be alone for a while. Can you stay with me until I doze off?" She scooted back against my chest and pulled my arm around her body.

I kissed her scalp. "You already know, you are my world and I would do anything for you. Plus, I miss holding you anyway on all of those times when Pops was on the road."

"Yeah, me too." She scooted back some more. Her hair was in my face. She smelled like Cherry Blossoms. "You know your father is right, don't you?"

"About what?" I rubbed her hip and held her tight.

"I will never feel like anybody is right for you. You are my little man and the only man that has ever loved me in the way that I needed to be loved. I don't wanna lose you. You belong to mama." She rolled all the way around until she was facing me. Her robe was mostly undone. "I love and I need you, Tyson." She kissed me and wrapped her arms around my neck.

"I'll always need you to, my Queen. You are my life." I wound up holding her until the sun came up in silence. When she finally drifted off to sleep, I kissed her forehead, and tucked her in? My mother was my life, beyond precious.

Chapter 14

Being that an intense war was taking place in Jamaica my Pops wound up staying in Kingston until he could see which way the war was heading. While he was doing his thing down there, he had troops back here in New York setting up shop getting ready to invade Harlem in a way that most drug lords had never seen their turfs invaded before.

My Pops had a date mapped out for when the invasion would take place, and he constantly sent word through me on how things were about to take place a week before my nineteenth birthday. While he remained in Jamaica, I took to training with some of his lethal assassins that were running back and forth between the island and New York doing what they did best which was killing shit.

Nine days before my nineteenth birthday, I ran into Ms. Jazzy coming out of Walmart with a shopping cart full of groceries. She was about to roll right past me until I called her name. She stopped and looked shielding her eyes from the sun. She had a blue three M doctor's mask on her face like everybody else had been wearing because of the Coronavirus that was going around.

I walked up to her with my arms partially opened. "What's good, Goddess?" It was bright, sunny, and breezy out and there were only a few clouds in the sky.

"Boy, you ain't heard how all of those people are getting sick and dying from that Coronavirus? They are running out of masks and everything? Where is yours?"

I shrugged my shoulders. "I don't know. Plus, I don't believe in that stuff. You betta give me my hug, though."

She smiled and walked into my arms. "You still got a thang for 'ol, Ms. Jazzy, huh?"

I trailed my hands around and cuffed her big booty. She was wearing a tight blue skirt dress and it felt like she ain't have no panties on. I liked that feeling. "You were my first. I'm always gon' have a crazy thing for you." A few cars cruised past us trying to find a space to park into. Because of the Coronavirus pandemic, the parking lot was full of cars. People were lined up along the side of Walmart. I had changed my mind about going inside.

Jazzy looked me up and down then snickered. "I know what you're saying but the way you're feeling is only going to get the both of us in trouble." She blushed and looked over my shoulder pulling her mask down so I could see those juicy lips.

"Yeah, you should already know that I ain't never been afraid of no trouble, especially when it comes to you." I gripped that ass some more and kissed her neck.

I don't know why but I had always had a weird thing for older women. I don't know if it was because of their maturity, or just because I had mommy issues, but whatever the case Ms. Jazzy had me feeling a sexual way about her which is odd because I had originally stopped her to find out where Tasia was. That was until I saw the way that ass jiggled in her skirt dress.

"You know what Tyson? Kammron is in D.C. for a few days. He and I ain't been seeing eye to eye no way, it's a long story. But what if you and I spent a night together just to get whatever this is out of our systems? What would you think about that?" She closed into me and kissed my lips, then she licked all over them and squeezed my dick through my jeans. "What you think about that?"

I groaned. My piece started to telescope right away. I wanted some of Ms. Jazzy bad, but at the same time, I was craving Tasia. Ms. Jazzy would have to wait until I figured out where things were going with her daughter. "That sounds like a plan but first I need you to tell me where Tasia is. I ain't heard from her in a few days and I'm worried about her."

Ms. Jazzy pursed her lips. "She's with Kammron. She has been with him for a week straight now. Everywhere he goes, she gotta go for some reason. I don't even wanna think about either one of them. I need some company. You wanna quarantine with me?"

There were so many questions I wanted to ask her in reference to Tasia but I decided against it. Clearly, Tasia was ignoring me. She hadn't answered any of my messages for nearly a week.

I squeezed Ms. Jazzy's ass tighter. "Let's go then I need to see what Kammron ain't been on."

* * *

Instead of heading to her house where she lived with both Kammron of the Coke Kings and Tasia her daughter, we decided to head to a hotel where Ms. Jazzy didn't waste any time. As soon as the door opened, she pulled me inside and began kissing all over my lips.

"Brang yo lil' young ass in here." She cuffed my dick and held it while she sucked on my neck. I nudged her off that. I already knew that Ashlynn was going to be checking my body for signs of infidelity, so I had to be smart. I didn't feel like hearing her mouth.

Ms. Jazzy closed the door and locked it. She stepped in front of me and pulled her skirt dress over her head. She dropped it to the floor. She had gained a little weight which fit her. She had a few stretch marks that went across her stomach and her thighs, she was thick. She reached into the front of her chest and unhooked her Victoria Secrets bra. Her brown breasts spilled out the nipples were already erect. She pulled her panties down next exposing her bushy pussy. That sight drove me crazy because that was some grown woman shit right there.

"Damn, you a fine ass mama. On everything, you killing shit, Ms. Jazzy." I picked her thick ass up.

She yelped, somehow my pants dropped, and my dick was out. I found her crease with a little maneuvering and then she was sliding down on it engulfing me with her heat.

"Damn, Mama." I sucked her neck and bounced her up and down.

"Mmm! Mmm! Mmm! Don't call me that, unnhhh!" She dug her nails into my shoulder blades.

"Uh! Uh! Call you what?" I bent my knees a little bit so I could continue throwing her up and down, she was leaking.

"Mama! That shit drives me crazy. Uh! Uh! I can't take it." She licked the left side of my face, then my ear.

I trembled. "This—my—pussy—Mama!" I growled and fell onto the bed with her. My hips rocked into her at full speed. She felt tighter, wetter and she was oozing all over me.

"Uh! Shit lil' boy! Shut up!" She locked her thighs around me and humped into me at full speed. She pulled me down and kissed my lips.

"Mama! Mama! Mama! Uhhh shit! Mama!" I knew it was getting to her because every time I said that word she shivered and jerked. "I'm yo' baby. You giving yo' baby dis pussy, right now!" I plunged at full speed, knocking at her bottom.

She screamed and came licking all over my ear. "I'm Mama. Me! Oh, fuck me!"

I pushed them thick thighs to her chest and watched my dick go in and out of her. Her dark brown lips were opened like a flower. Juices sped out of the hole and into her ass crack while my balls slammed against it. Her scent rose to my nostrils, and it drove me nuts. This was my first piece of pussy, and she was allowing me to live out a crazy fantasy while I was deep in that box. I could barely contain myself.

She opened her thighs wide and watched me pound her out. "Uhhhh! Uhhhh! Shit! Baby, it's yours! Mama, say it's yours!" She arched her back hard and came again. She pulled me down and ran her nails across my back, drawing blood.

"Aww shit!" I pushed her ass against the bed.

She rolled from under me and straddled me. She grabbed my dick and put it back into herself. "You wanna be my baby. Okay, den, let mama ride her baby den." She sunk down and rolled her hips while I held onto her big booty.

I watched her sexy stomach. The stretch marks turned me on even more because it was like they were proof that she really was a mother. For some reason that made me harder. This was a vet, and her pussy was good. She bounced up and down on me with her head tilted backward. Drool slipped out of the corners of her mouth.

"Say it. Uh! Uh! Uh, shit! Say it, baby!"

My eyes were rolled into the back of my head. I didn't snap out of my blissful zone until she slapped me across the face and screamed that she needed to hear it.

"Hear what?" She was bouncing up and down in my lap as only a vet could. That pussy was getting better and better. "Hear what?"

"Call—me—Mommy!" She tilted her head back and really started riding me?

Sweat dripped off her chin and onto my chest. My fingers slipped into her ass crack. My middle digit went into her back door.

"Mama, you fuckin' yo baby. You nasty!" I sat up and forced her to take me deeper.

She screamed and bit into my neck riding me so fast that all I could do was whimper. "Cum in me, baby. Cum in mama! Please!"

I rolled her over when I felt myself getting ready to cum and went deep inside of her. I started to jerk, and my seed began to fly. She yelped and hugged me tightly calling me her baby. I came and came. She rolled from under me and took a hold of my dick sucking her juices from it.

"Boy—" She popped me out. "I don't know how you bring dat crazy shit out of me when you be talking that shit, but you do. I watched him grow up from this high and sometimes I'm so sick that I imagine you really are my baby. Am I wrong?" She sucked me into her mouth.

I grabbed the sheets and shook my head. "N'all, I imagined that, too. Ain't nobody gotta know what we are thinking. That shit felt so good."

She climbed back on top of me and slid me back into her gap. She sat all the way back and looked down on me. "Kammron said that my stomach looks disgusting. He said when I'm on top of him like this, I should cover my stomach. What do you think and be honest?"

I rolled her once again and pulled out of her. I climbed between her thighs and kissed all over her stomach. "This stomach is perfect. You got these badges of honor from giving birth. That makes you a mother." I trembled and licked all over her stomach. Every time I felt one of the stretch mark ridges, I wanted to cum. I rubbed my face on her tummy and slid back into her.

"Uh! He says I got them on my breasts, too."

"Shit, you do." I was stroking her moderately.

"Do they make me ugly?" She ran her tongue all over her lips.

I licked her tongue and sucked her lips into my mouth. "Makes you a Queen. Now give dat shit to yo' baby." She shook. "If you were my baby you would never leave my room. I swear to God!" She wrapped her arms around me whimpering in my ear.

I plunged her at full speed until I came again. Then we French kissed for twenty straight minutes. She rode me until she came again and grew weak. She wound up falling asleep on my chest. I held her, I felt remorseful but only slightly. I had a thing for Ms. Jazzy. I didn't know how I was going to shake it.

When I woke up early the next morning, she was rubbing my abs and kissing each one of my nipples individually. She smiled as soon as my focus turned to her. "Hey, baby. How was your sleep?"

I nodded. "Good."

She climbed on top of me. "I'm gon' need you from time to time Tyson and I don't want to argue with you about this." She kissed my lips and slowly licked them. "You don't have any idea how important it is for a woman my age to have somebody like you ducked off in the cut. You make me feel so good about myself. I feel perfect and I already know that I am far from it. Men lust for me when I am wearing these clothes but when I take them off and they see my slight imperfections it makes them look at me differently. At least Kammron does." She was quiet, she looked dreamy-eyed. Then she sighed and shook her head as if to knock herself out of her daze.

I had that booty and I was rubbing all over it. It felt so hot and the fact that it was attached to an older woman was enough to make me wanna go in her again. "Yo' excuse my French but fuck ya' baby daddy, Jazzy. Word up, dat nigga is a clown. Any man that can't look at this maternal body right here and appreciate it, especially after you done popped out his kids need a young nigga like me to knock him out the box and wax this thang on the low. I don't know what's good wit' Kammron but I would love it if my woman had my seeds and she snapped back like this. Word to Jehovah man."

She leaned down. "I wish I had yo' lil' fine ass walking around my house every day all day. I swear I woulda never been able to keep my hands off you. Men ain't the only ones that be on that freaky shit, especially when you make a woman feel like you're making me feel right now." She looked into my eyes. "So, when I call you will you come to me?"

"Yo' before I say yeah, I need you to know that me and Tasia feel some type of way for each other. I think I love her and all that shit. If I don't I think I am damn close. I just gotta be honest."

"Oh, yeah?" She grabbed my hard piece and slid it into her hot folds. She scooted back on it and engulfed me with her eyes closed. "You think my daughter can do you like I can, Tyson?" She slowly rode me and used her inner walls to squeeze me off and on.

My eyelids fluttered, I felt like one of my eyes were going lazy. That felt so good. "Nah, I ain't saying that. Uh! Uh, Mama." I held her ass while she rode me some more. She sucked on my neck. She rode me fast and hard. I jerked ready to cum. My fingers dug into the flesh of her ass. Right before I was about to cum, she hopped off me.

She played with herself until she came. Then she sucked her fingers clean. She stood at the edge of the bed. "You can feel what you feel for Tasia. Tyson, that's cool, but I'm letting you know right now Kammron would rather kill you or any other boy before they are able to get a hold of Tasia. He got her ass locked down. He cares about her more now than he does me. So, you can roll the dice if you want to but I am sure that you are going to come out on the losing end." She started to get dressed, with a look of irritation on her face. "I'm out of here."

I jumped out of the bed and held her. "Ms. Jazzy, I'll be there. You got my word on that." I hugged her body to mine.

T.J. Edwards

Chapter 15

When I got home that morning, Hermés was on her way out of the house while I was on my way in. She shook her head and grunted with her car keys in her hand. The sun's rays shined off her greasy forehead. "Uh-huh, yo' monka ass taking the walk of shame." She laughed and chirped the alarm to her Dodge Durango. She opened the door and got in it before I could even respond.

I stepped into the house, the first thing I smelled was breakfast. I could hear something frying in a skillet. I walked further into the house. Ashlynn came out of the linen closet. When she saw me, she stopped dead in her tracks and lowered her eyes. She was carrying a few hand towels. She lifted them into the air and slammed them to the ground. She stormed out of the hallway, past the kitchen and into the basement.

I picked up the towels and placed them back into the linen closet closing the door. I stepped into the kitchen and my mother was standing at the stove cooking. I crept behind her, wrapped my arms around her waist, and kissed her soft cheek. "Hey, beautiful?"

She leaned further back into me. "Hey?"

"I'm smelling all this good food and stuff. Are you making yo' baby some?"

"Maybe. Depends on if you're going to ask me or not?" She tried to look back at me.

I kissed her cheek. "I miss yo' cooking, it's been a while."

"I got you." She turned all the way around and held my face while she looked into my eyes. "That girl is hurt. I don't know where you have been, or what you've been doing but she is assuming the worst. Be careful, Jamaican women are very vindictive." She kissed me and hugged my neck.

"Thank you, my Queen." I grabbed a sausage out of the pan and she popped me on the shoulder.

I hurried out of the back door and closed it. I bit a piece of the sausage and enjoyed the seasonings on it before I headed down the stairs toward Ashlynn.

She was sitting on the couch with her thighs crossed, rubbing lotion into her hands. "Who is she?"

I came off the last step. "What are you talking about?"

She glared at me. "Stop playin' wit me, Tyson. You have been gone for eighteen hours. You ain't picked up yo' phone to call me and you ain't checked in with nobody in this house. Who is the bitch that you were with last night all the way up until this fuckin' morning?" She cracked her knuckles and took her earrings out of her ears. "Was it Tasia's lil' black ass, huh? Were you wit' that burnt ass bitch?"

"Man, watch yo' mafuckin' mouth. Black is beautiful, I thought you knew that."

"So, it was her. You actually cheated on me with her? Really, Tyson?" She stood up with tears coming down her face already. "How could you do me like that, huh?"

"Yo' you bugging, I ain't never said I was with a female. Yo' lil' ass is just game conscious." I took off my shirt and threw it in the hamper. Then I pulled off my white beater.

Ashlynn took a deep breath and stepped back pointing at me. "You bitch ass nigga. You got the nerve to have all these scratches on your back? Are you kidding me, right now?" She rushed over to me and grabbed my chin. "Look at your fuckin' neck! Look at it!" She muffed me hard.

I stumbled and wound up in front of the mirror looking over the passion marks Ms. Jazzy had given me. My neck was horrible. She had definitely marked her territory and she was too mature to have not known what she was doing. She meant to get me in trouble, and she had succeeded in her mission.

"I got into a fight wit' some niggas that was trying to jump Maze. I ain't finna never let my nigga get jumped. Fuck that."

"Save it. Maze was here looking for you twice already." She pointed her finger in my face. "Nigga I swear to God you better stop playin' wit' me like I'm some punk or somethin'. I might be a female, but my balls are as big as yours. Trust me on that." She poked me on the forehead with her finger.

Since I was in the wrong, I took that on the chin. "Yo' I ain't cheat. I ain't got no reason to cheat on you. You are a good ass woman with hella shit between ya' legs."

"Yet and still you go out and defile our marital bed. You disgust me." She pushed me with both hands and brushed past me. She took a seat on the bed and crossed her thighs again. "I hope that bitch was worth the respect that you just lost from me."

I waved her off. "Fuck what you talkin' 'bout. I told you I got into a scuffle. You can believe what you believe. I ain't finna sit here and try to convince you of nothing. Take it how you want to." I grabbed some clothes so I could get into the shower.

"So, since we have been together. I suppose you have never lied to me, huh?"

I wracked my brain quickly. Outside of this lie, and it was a doozy, I didn't think I had ever lied to her. At least I didn't think that she had any proof that I did. "I ain't lying to you now, and I ain't never lied to you."

She laughed. "Oh, really?"

"Yeah, Ashlynn, really."

She stood up. "Do you know why King is over in Jamaica warring so hard against the Deadly Guerillas? Huh, do you?"

"N'all, why?" I stopped at the bottom of the steps on my way up them.

"Because the footage from the Jamaican Carnival came back and you are seen gunning down Manifest, then running to one of King's cars. Cameras throughout Jamaica followed the car until it got to the hotel. You waited until you got out of it to remove your mask. You were identified as the shooter. The war is on and it's all because of your ignorance. Plus, that makes it the first lie that you told to me."

I felt light-headed. Was she telling the truth or simply trying to call my bluff? I didn't know but I felt sick imagining those turn of events. "I don't know who told you that shit but it ain't true. Anyway, I'm about to hit this water." I headed up the stairs.

"Tyson, come here." Ashlynn hustled to the bottom of the stairs. "Bring yo' ass down here, right now!"

I stopped and turned around. "What's up?"

"Come here." She pointed at the ground.

I came back down the stairs and stood in front of her. "What's good?"

She slowly trailed her eyes upward until they were looking into my own. "I demand the truth. I am your wife under God. We are one flesh and so far, you have chained me to your infidelity. I need you to be a man and admit that you cheated, tell me why." She stepped closer into my face. I could smell her Apple scented shampoo. "Do it now."

I sighed. "I ain't got shit to say. I ain't fucked off on you. If I would have, I would just tell you. We both know that we got forced into this shit. Ain't no sense in faking the funk? I care about you, but this marriage is foogazy. Now I'm going to shower.

She nodded her head. "And so, the man shall reap what he has sown. Hell hath no fury like a woman scorned. I curse your behavior. This pain you too shall know. I promise you this." She turned away and walked off.

136

I stood there for a moment stuck. I wanted to tell her the truth. I wanted to get the shit over with but for some reason, I couldn't bring myself to do it. I felt that if I admitted it that I would box myself into a corner where my power would be scarce. By lying there had to be at the very least a shred of doubt within her that believed I was telling the truth. Even if it wasn't I felt like only a damn fool would snitch on himself.

***

Later that night Hermés called me into her room. When I stepped inside, she closed the door and sat on the bed. Her room was illuminated by candles. "Tyson, I need to tell you something and I don't want you to freak out."

By her saying this it only allowed me to freak out. I stood in front of her with a frown on my face. "Man, what's good?"

"See you're already getting angry. I can't even tell you. I don't want you judging me right now because I really need a shoulder to cry on."

I took a deep breath and sat down beside her. I didn't want to spook her or stop her from telling me what was on her mind. "Talk to me, sis."

"A'ight; as long as this is a safe space. Is it?" She looked up at me.

"Of course, it is. You can tell me anything. Go ahead." Her candles smelled like Vanilla.

"I made a mistake when I was depressed and at my lowest point." She exhaled loudly and shook her head. "Tyson, I fucked up and tried Heroin. Now, I can't get that shit out of my system." She hugged herself. "I've been doing it for a few weeks, and I feel like I need it every second of every day. I don't know what to do."

I slapped her so hard that I regretted doing it as soon as I had. She fell to the floor, landing on her knees. "You say you tried what?" I stood over her.

Hermés crawled around on the floor trying to get a hold of herself. She whimpered, "I know it was stupid, but I am hurting so bad. I have pains going on inside me that you will never understand." She slowly came to her feet holding her face.

"I can't believe you, Hermés? Why didn't you just come and talk to me? Why would you try that shit knowing that it can hook you worse than any other drug?"

"I don't know, Tyson. But it's been helping. I feel so strong now. I can't feel the pain, I don't think about the agony when I am on it. All I can think about is bliss."

Agony from what? I needed to know. "What is going on? Tell me."

Just then my mother knocked on Hermés' bedroom door and stuck her head in. "Tyson, Tasia is at the door. She says that she needs to see you. That it is an emergency."

Chapter 16

When I stepped onto the stoop, Tasia had her back to the door with her arms crossed around her body. She rubbed her shoulders while her yellow and blue sundress blew in the wind. She turned around to face me with a blue mask over her face. I guessed just like everybody else that was going crazy over the Coronavirus she was doing the same as well by taking the preventive measure of covering her nose and mouth.

"Hey."

"What's good, girl?" I opened my arms and waited until she walked inside of them. She hugged me, and I hugged her back. "What's with this mask shit?"

"I ain't trying to catch that stuff. The death toll is constantly rising out here in New York. I gotta be safe." She stepped back and placed a tuft of hair behind her ear. "I'm sorry for just dropping in on you like this but I really needed to talk to you."

"It's all good, sit down." I dusted off the top stair of the stoop and helped her take a seat. It was a bright and sunny day. There was a light wind flowing from East to West, and the sky was a pretty blue with a few clouds in it.

Tasia took a seat and made sure that she was flashing anybody that coulda walked past. She pulled down her sundress as much as she could then sighed. "I wanna kill my daddy, Tyson."

I sat down beside her. "Why would you wanna do that?"

"It's a long story. Let's just say that Kammron really ain't my biological father. He's been there ever since I was one, and he's pretty much the only father that I know, but he isn't my biological dad." The wind blew and this caused her hair to blow along with it.

"Okay, so is that the reason you wanna kill him?" I didn't see that being a good enough reason to do the do with Kammron.

"Ever since he's been home. Hell; ever since I was thirteen-years-old he's been going in on me and doing things to me that no father should ever do to his little girl. You see, Kammron doesn't even go there sexually with my mother anymore because he has stated his claim on me."

I jerked my head back. "So, what you sayin'? You been fuckin' this nigga?"

She lowered her head. "Kammron is a beast. He has a bunch of cold-hearted trap and jack boys running under him. He isn't the type of man that you can say no to. I knew this ever since I was old enough to form my first words."

"So, then that is a yes. You have been fuckin' him."

She nodded. "I haven't had any other choice." She sighed. "My mother caught us in the act an hour ago. She showed back up at home and I was under him while he was doing his thing to me. I didn't wanna do it, but he made me. I hate myself so much that I don't know what to do, right now." She rested her face in her arms that were over her lap.

A cherry red Cadillac Escalade rolled down the street with its music blaring. The sun reflected off the good rims.

My mind was spinning. I started thinking about all the things I had done with Ms. Jazzy last night and all that morning. Had it not been her daughter Ms. Jazzy really wouldn't have had the right to be angry at Kammron. "So, why are you here?"

"I needed somebody to talk to. You're the only one that I know I can talk to. I am praying that you don't look at me differently, right now. Do you?"

I shook my head. "Never that. You can't control what that grown ass nigga's do. But then again you are a woman now.

You aren't a little kid anymore like when you were thirteen and he was going in on you. Why don't you just run away from him and never return?"

"Because I am supposed to come to him when he summons me. He said that if ever he calls me, and I don't break my neck to get to him when he catches me, he is going to break it anyway. I believe him, Kammron is crazy." A tear ran down her cheek and she wiped it away.

I scooted closer and placed my arm around her shoulder. "Tasia, I got you. You ain't ever gotta go back around dat nigga if you don't want too. I got some ends put up. I can help you get a crib over in another borough. Hell, you can move to Brooklyn and I'll front you until you can get on your feet."

"Boy you really don't watch the news, do you?" She looked over at me.

"Not really, I get all my updates from Facebook. Why you say it like that?"

"Because Tyson, they are talking about putting a stay at home order in place. There is already a social distancing order from the Governor. They are saying that you're not supposed to be within six feet of another person. Technically how close we are sitting to each other we could get fined."

I smacked my lips. "Man fuck them. So, what are you going to do then, you finna go home?"

"I can't my mother put me out and she isn't letting me get none of my stuff. Luckily, I had a few dollars so I could jump on the subway. Now I am here. You think I can chill here with you for a couple of days? At least until I can figure some things out?"

I thought about that for a moment. I imagined how I would convince Ashlynn and every scenario that I came up with in my mind just didn't play out right. "You know I got this Jamaican wife and Shorty is wild. I chilled out last night and she already thought that I was out with you. I wouldn't even know what to say to her, or how to ask her that question."

Tasia nodded. "Yeah, I get it." She exhaled loudly again. "Guess I gotta figure this shit out on my own then." She stood up.

I could smell her perfume mixed with her deodorant. I stood up beside her. "Let me give you some money for a hotel." I pulled out a knot of fifties and gave her three hundred dollars.

She took the six fifties and smiled. "Thank you, Tyson. I wish things were different. It seems like you are always coming through for me." She hugged me tightly. "I wish we could be together, but friendship is just as nice I guess."

My arms went around her waist and I held her. "I'm crazy about you Tasia whether you know it or not. I might have done some crazy things lately but I swear to God I am crazy about you."

"I'm crazy about you, too. I've been crazy about you ever since I was little. You know that we are supposed to be together, don't you? Nobody makes me feel how you make me feel when we hug. Every time your arms wrap around me, I feel so safe, so secure, so in love. I need you, Tyson. I swear I do." She hugged me tighter.

I closed my eyes while I held her. She felt perfect, her warmth, her scent, her feel, her height. All of it was perfect for me. I wanted Tasia. "I'ma put you up in a hotel, then I'm coming to see you. I need to be with you, right now. I feel so lost. How about the Best Western over on Lincoln?"

"Okay." She stepped back and looked into my eyes. "You saved my life. I will never forget that. I owe myself to you." She leaned in and kissed my lips before I could even think about what to do. Her lips crashed into mine and she sucked all over them ever so softly.

I held her firmer and eased into the display of affection. She moaned, and so did I. My tongue crept into her mouth and seemed to create a slow dance with her own.

"Aw hell, n'all! See, now you really got me fucked up!" Ashlynn rushed us and pulled me away from Tasia, then she slapped me across the face so hard that I wound up against the banister. She jumped into Tasia's mug. "First you stay out all night fuckin' my man and now you're sitting here on the porch kissing all over him like he ain't got a whole ass wife in the house? Fuck is wrong wit' chu?"

Tasia took a step back and held her hands up at shoulder level. "I don't know what you're talking about as far as him staying out all night because he wasn't with me. As far as that kiss goes, I apologize for that. We were in the moment and I just went for it. I've always had a thing for Tyson, and he knows that." She looked over at me.

I was still trying to gather myself. Ashlynn was heavy-handed as hell.

"You think I give a fuck about what you got for my husband? Bitch, I am his wife. He belongs to me and I will kill yo' black ass over him with no hesitation. Now keep yo' fuckin' distance away from him or else."

Tasia frowned. "Yo' ain't ho hoez over here ma'. This is Harlem. We can do whatever you wanna do. I'm just sayin'."

Ashlynn came out of her waistband with a blade. The sunlight reflected off the steel of it. She cocked back her arm ready to swing it forward to slice Tasia across the face. I grabbed her arm and pulled her back to me.

Tasia jumped back and held her face. "Dat bitch was finna cut me?" She looked shocked.

"Let me go so I cyaan kill dis rude gyal. Mi don't know what she tink dis is." The strong Kingston accent came out of her. She kicked her legs wildly.

I tightened my grip on her wrist so she could drop the knife. After doing this for a full minute she dropped it.

Tasia backed up on the sidewalk. "I'm going to that place, Tyson. I'll see you when I see you." She started to walk down the block. The further she went away from me the more I wanted her. I didn't know why I craved her so bad, but I did.

Ashlynn twisted in my arms like crazy until she remained still. I held her until I knew that Tasia was long gone. Then I released her. She slapped me again and picked up her knife. Her eyes were bright green. She threw open the door and snapped. "Get in the house, now!"

"Who the fuck you think you talking too?" I grabbed her by her shirt and balled it into my left fist I was ready to punch her yellow ass. My cheek was stinging like a mafucka, and I wasn't with nobody getting shots off on me, not even my wife.

Ashlynn held her head down. "Tyson Jean, get your ass in the house so we can talk. Please." She stared at me.

"That's moe like it." I looked around and saw that the entire neighborhood seemed like they were watching us. I held the door open for her. She looked up at me while she walked into the house and stormed right into the basement.

When I got down there, she was pacing back and forth. I could tell that she was on the verge of losing her temper. "Tyson, what do you take me for? Do you think that just because I am from Jamaica that I am stupid, or ignorant, huh? Do you think that I don't deserve the right to have a man be faithful to me?"

"Ashlynn, I apologize for what you walked out there and saw. That shit just happened. You out there acting all ghetto and shit, though. Pulling knives out like you done lost yo' damn mind."

She walked up to me. "Had you not have stopped me I would have made her so ugly that nobody would have ever wanted her again. In Jamaica, the wife will not spare her wrath on the mistress. Her life is ticking away. You can't hold me back forever." She licked the blade of the knife and put it back on her person.

"So, now all of a sudden you love me? You're willing to kill a bitch over me because you care about me that much?" I needed to know where she was coming from because these emotions were up and down. She was all over the place. I didn't know how I felt about her. I still felt too young and immature to be able to make a decision.

"Wives submit to your husbands as the weaker vessel. Respect him. Sarah called her husband Lord even though she didn't agree with a lot of his actions. You are my husband under God. You belong to me. Your body is not your own. So, you muthafuckin' right I will kill Tasia over you. You are mine." She was in my face now. Her breath smelled like Double mint gum.

I placed my forehead to hers. "I'm not there yet. I care about her, and you. Me and Tasia were starting to get our lives on track before I was forced into this marriage. I don't know where things might have gone but this arranged marriage ruined all of those chances but not our feelings."

"You think this works for me? Huh, Tyson, you think I like the fact that I was forced to marry a man that I didn't even know? A man that killed my best friend and then lied about it to my face. Have you stopped to think how I am feeling, right now?"

"Nope, because that ain't my problem. Fuck Jamaica and all those weak ass practices. I didn't ask for this shit and I ain't finna submit to it either. As far as I am concerned, we are only married in Jamaica. I ain't signed shit no way. I don't even know if the marriage is valid."

Ashlynn walked into my face. "Do you deny me as your wife? That's all I need to know?"

I searched her green eyes that were slowly turning back hazel. She looked vulnerable yet angry. She was undeniably beautiful. I couldn't deny that. "Damn."

She backed up. "Take some time and ask yourself that question. I need to think. I'ma see if Hermés will let me use her car. I'll see you later."

When she walked away, I sat on the bed with my face in between my hands. "Fuck man, why is this shit so hard?" I hollered.

I needed to figure my life out. I had to make a decision soon. Time was wearing out and feelings were becoming more and more serious on each end. I didn't want to hurt Tasia and I didn't want to continue to hurt Ashlynn. I needed to man up and choose.

Chapter 17

Maybe it was out of stupidity, or maybe I was just hardheaded, but I met up with Tasia three hours later at the Best Western hotel. When I got to the room door, she opened it and took a step back for me to come in. She was dressed in a pair of gray and pink boy shorts with a belly shirt that read Pink on the front of it.

"Come on in, Tyson."

I walked into the room still feeling like I didn't know if I was making the right decision. "Shorty, I don't know why I am here. I guess a part of me just really needed to see you."

She smiled and backed up closing the door at the same time. "I have been missing you like crazy. Ever since I left your house all I have been thinking about is the fact that you have saved my life for a second time and that I just wanna lay in the bed and hug up with you."

I walked up to her and kissed her lips. "I like the sound of that." I held her head with my big hands and tongued her down.

Her lips were juicy. Her want was lustful. She moaned into my mouth and ran her small hands up and down my back. She pulled me closer to her. I broke our embrace, I could feel my dick getting hard.

"Tasia, ain't this kind of weird? You know, after all that shit that's been going down with Kammron?"

She looked up at me. "Are you asking me if every time we touch does it repulse me? If you are then the answer is no, I like you a lot Tyson. I hope whatever we do here tonight doesn't have to result in sex, especially because while I was getting off of the Subway on my way here, I started to cramp. It's about time for my cycle to come down and I don't want our first time to be a disaster." She laughed shortly.

I nodded. "Long as you know that I do desire you, and I most definitely wanna tap this ass but you are worth more than that to me. We can just chill. I would love to listen to your heart."

She balanced her foot from one to the other. "Are you serious?"

"Yeah, Baby, why not?" I took her small hand and led her to the bed.

"Kammron told me that it was a woman's job to make a man feel good at all times. He used to make me run his bathwater and rub lotion onto his feet for as long as I could remember. He was the one that gave me baths from the time that I was three on up to ten. I don't know why my mother didn't figure out that once a child becomes five years old that they can wash themselves. Even more than that, a man should never be able to bathe a girl. I don't care if it is his child or not."

She backed up into me. "Tyson, I think you are going to be a really great father. You know, whenever Ashlynn does get pregnant and have your child. I am sure that if it's a girl that you will treat her like a princess. You have this way about you when it comes to attention and detail of a woman that just makes sense. My mother has even said good things about you. Before all of this happened, she used to call you her son. I didn't even know that the two of you were that close."

She rolled around until she was facing me. Her small hand held my face. "What do you wanna be when you finally step off the stoop? Are you going to be a drug lord like your father King, or are you going to be a hardworking man that provides for his family and makes sure that everybody is taken care of at all times by legit means?"

"To be honest with you, Tasia. I ain't thought about none of that. The only thing I think about every day is breaking free from my father and getting to a place where I can be my own man. I can't see myself following behind him or taking orders from him for the rest of my life. I am my own man."

"I know you are. And when you get this freedom what kind of life do you see? Is there a wife, are there children, or are you a Playboy with limitless women?" Her thumb traced my eyebrows.

"I see you there. Me and you, I don't know the level of our relationship, but I see you by my side. What about you?"

"You can't do anything in life without money. So, I know that whatever I do it has to make a nice amount of money. As far as my family life goes—" She sighed. "I just want to be loved and appreciated. I want a husband that will only see me. I want God-fearing, obedient children that honor both myself and my husband. I see a suburban four-bedroom house, two-car garage, a minivan, and a luxury vehicle. Soccer games and PTA meetings. That would be the perfect life for me."

"Do you see me there?" Our noses were touching, I could feel the heat of her breath on my face.

"As crazy as it may sound, I sure do. I feel like when it's all said and done that you and I will be together against all odds. I think I love you already, Tyson. You saved my life, twice." She stroked my cheek and held me around the neck with her forearm.

"I love you, too." I couldn't believe the words had left my mouth, but they did, and I honestly felt like that about Tasia even though I only scarcely understood love in its every form.

"You mean that?" Her forehead pressed more firmly against my own.

"Yeah, I do." I kissed her lips. She purred and closed her eyes.

She felt so good lying there in front of me. Her heat. Her presence. Tasia made my heart feel a way that it had never felt before. I kissed her forehead. "Yo' hand to God, I'ma kill that nigga Kammron if he ever touches you again. That nigga is a predator, and somebody needs to crush his bitch ass."

She opened her eyes. "That's how I feel about Ashlynn even though I know I don't have any right to be feeling like that. She is your wife. But I want you all to myself, Tyson. I need you all to myself. I've never been shown real love. No one has ever taken the time out to love me in the way that a girl or even a woman is supposed to be loved. I know that you can. I know that you will. I am willing to fight for your love."

"If a man makes you fight for his love it isn't real. The love that I have for you I don't even understand it. All I know is that I am crazy about you and I am ready to kill a nigga over you with no hesitation. Kammron is on my hit list."

She shivered. "You would really kill somebody over me?"

"Hell yeah."

She got up and straddled my body placing one thick thigh on each side of my waist. She positioned herself so that her pussy was right over my covered pipe. She opened her thighs further to feel me better, then she laid her head on my chest. "I never had a man say that he would kill for me before. The things you be saying sometimes mentally does somethin' to me that I can barely comprehend. It's like I want and need you so freaking bad. I know that if you were my man I would hold you down like no other."

I placed my hands on her ass, I couldn't help it. Tasia was so strapped. I rubbed all over that booty looking into her eyes. "When I break away from King it's going to be me and you. I have been feeling you ever since we were shorties. Now that we are grown I gotta have you for my woman but there are two people standing in our way and both feel like they have a major say in our lives and what we do. We need to break away from them."

"Baby, isn't it three people because what about Ashlynn? Do you even care about her, be honest?"

I had to think about that for a moment. Whenever I was with Ashlynn, I felt a sense of peace yet anxiety at the same time. She felt good in my arms but there were times when I was wishing that she was Tasia whereas whenever I was with Tasia I never wished that she was Ashlynn. Ashlynn also made me think about King and my bondage by Jamaica. I didn't know if Ashlynn would ever enact her revenge on me for the thing that I had done to Manifest but that was always in the back of my mind. But I did care about her because I could tell that she genuinely cared about me.

"Yeah, I care about her. Ashlynn is a good woman. She says she cares about me and I believe her."

Tasia sat up and then back. "Then why are you here? Why not just be with her?" She sounded and looked defeated. Her shoulders were slumped. She avoided eye contact with me until she grew the nerve to look into my eyes while I answered her question.

"Because she doesn't have my heart. I don't know how you got it, but you do."

Tasia smiled and dimples appeared on both of her cheeks. "I better have it." She laid back down. "So, how are we going to break away from them?"

I started to rub that ass again. "That's a good question, baby. Give me a few days to figure that out. Cool?"

"That sounds good to me. Now can you hold me for a few hours before you gotta get back to her?"

"Yeah, I got you, boo."

***

T.J. Edwards

When I came into the house that night it was midnight, and Hermés had just gotten in because she was still taking off her shoes. She had on a pair of sunglasses. She licked her lips and staggered trying to walk up and hug me. I could tell that she was faded. "Hey, baby brother. How was your day?" She slurred and scratched the inner forearm.

I took hold of her shoulders. "Yo' sis, are you high?"

She smiled and tried to buck her eyes open as far as they could go. "N'all Tyson, I'm good. Why do you ask me that?" She balanced herself as best as she could.

I put my arm around her neck and helped her get to her bedroom. I opened the door and she walked into it and began taking her clothes off until she was sitting on the edge of the bed in just her bra and panties. She grabbed bottled water from her nightstand and started drinking from it.

I came and kneeled before her. "Hermés, what is wrong with you?"

She ran her fingers through her hair and closed her eyes leaning all the way to the side. "Ain't nothing wrong with me, bruh. I'm just feeling a bit under the weather, that's all." She scratched her arm again. She squeezed her eyelids shut and leaned forward on the couch until her forehead was touching her knees. She began to snore, then she jerked her head up as if she was missing somethin'.

I stood up, I was hurt. "Sis, who got you to fuckin' wit' this shit? Tell me."

She snored for fifteen seconds. She jerked awake and scratched her arm for a full minute. She smacked her lips. "Dis is Brooklyn. Everybody and they mama doing Heroin, especially since the Coronavirus is forcing people to be quarantined." She rubbed the back of her neck. "You don't love me no more, huh?" She laughed and her face immediately scrunched up. She broke down crying. "I'm sick, Tyson. I got

152

H.I.V. and I don't know what to do." She fell from the bed and landed on her knees.

My knees buckled. "You got what?"

She was crying hard, nodding. "You heard me. It's all I think about every second of every day. I think I am driving myself crazy thinking about it so much." She got up suddenly. "I need another fix." She walked to her dresser and pulled out her Heroin kit.

Next thing I knew, she was boiling the Heroin on a spoon. Before she drew it up with a syringe, she rubbed an alcohol pad on her inner forearm over the veins. She took the syringe and slid it into her. She drew back the feeder. The syringe filled with her blood and the drug then she pressed down on the feeder until it all disappeared inside of her. She pulled the needle out and licked her inner forearm. My mind was blown. She sat still for a moment and then she began to lean all the way to her left so hard that it looked like she was about to tip over.

"Who gave you this shit, sis? Tell me, please?"

She shook her head. That snitching shit ain't in me, Tyson. Plus, if I told you who gave me this you wouldn't believe me. Nobody can be trusted. This world is full of sick ass people that destroy and kill. It's a damn shame when you're dealt an unfair hand and there is nothing that you can do about it!" She sat crossed-legged on the floor now with her eyes closed. Seconds later she was leaning and snoring again.

I stood there speechless. I didn't know what to do, or what to say. Hermés was my sister and it was my job to protect her against all odds but there was no way for me to do this. I felt weak. I wanted to save her. I was praying that she was overreacting.

She opened her eyes. "Trust nobody, expect evil from everybody. I never even had a chance. I swear to God I didn't. Get out of my room, Tyson. I need to be alone."

I dropped to my knees and pulled her to me. Tears were streaming down my cheeks. "Who did this to you, Hermés. Tell me? Which one of these bitch ass niggas gave you this disease?" I shook her.

She cried and wiped the snot from her nose. "I never had a chance. Now get out of my room." She frowned her face. "Go! Now! Get out! I wanna be alone. Father in heaven wanna be alone."

I stood outside of her door in the hallway feeling helpless. Was it my fault that my sister had contracted this disease? Could I have prevented it? Was it somebody close to us that had given it to her? What did she mean by trust nobody and expect evil from everybody? Did she mean from me as well? All these thoughts were going through my mind when Ashlynn came out of the basement and walked right up to me.

"I found Odana? She is here in New York. You have to go with me to get her. I know that we are not on the best terms, right now, but I really need your help." She closed her hand together in prayer fashion.

"A'ight, give me a second to gather myself and we can leave." I slid down the wall until I was sitting down.

My head lowered, I was lost. I felt like Hermés was slipping through my fingers and I didn't know what to do in order to get a firm grasp on her. One thing was for sure and that was, I was going to get to the bottom of who had been the culprit to give my sister this disease. Once I found out who they were I was dead set on crushing the enemy.

Chapter 18

Ashlynn said that she had found out that her sister Odana was living in a two-story, red-bricked house out in Queens, New York. When she read the address to me it didn't ring any bells. I was unfamiliar with the territory and was sure that the neighborhood was a good one. It was an unusual rainy night with lightning flashing across the sky in thick bolts. The rain pelted down on my windshield like hail. I had the wipers on high and that was the only noise going on inside the car except the noise from the tires driving through the water on the streets that had already accumulated. We must've rolled for nearly twenty-five minutes before I broke the silence.

"I apologize for all the stuff I've taken you through since you've been up here from Jamaica. I know you didn't ask to come here and that you deserve better than what I've been giving you. After we get your sister back, I think it would be necessary for us to get an understanding amongst ourselves. The last thing I want you to have is any ill feelings toward me. I mean I do care about you."

She sucked her teeth. "You had me until you said that dumb shit. All the apologies and you standing up and being man enough to admit your faults all that was admirable until you said the last part about caring for me. There is no way that a man can care about a woman and treat me like you've done. All I need is for you to help me get Odana back tonight. I will hide her, and when we get enough money then I will find a way for us to make it to Haiti where my uncle is. He will accept us with open arms."

"So, you're half Haitian?" Maybe that was why her eyes changed so many colors and she was so exotic looking.

Ashlynn turned to me. "Tyson, I know you are just trying to find words to fill in the blanks while we're traveling. Your conscious is getting the better of you, and you don't know what to do about it, but I assure you that I am well. I will be okay. Help me get my sister back and you and I can fake it until we find a way to break away from each other. We can make this a business relationship until we accomplish the greater good for each of us individually. How does that sound to you?"

"Man, fuck that. You sitting yo' high yella ass over there acting like you ain't got no feelings for me when I know that is the furthest thing from the truth. Now I can admit when I am wrong, and I have been. But at the same time, I am not perfect. I really do care about you, and I wish things were different. I hate the fact that I was already feeling a way for Tasia before you came into the picture. It's not fair to you because you are forced to conform to my life after being stripped out of your own comfort. Why can't we sit down and try and get an understanding about all of this? I don't wanna be your enemy."

"You're not my enemy, Tyson. I don't look at you like that so you can calm down. Dang." She looked out of her window.

I rolled for a full block before I asked the question that was plaguing me. "Well, how do you look at me then?"

"Like you're the man that has me eight weeks pregnant." She said this and kept looking out of the window.

It took me a second to actually digest what she'd just said. When I did my head jerked backward. "Wait, are you saying that we are going to have a baby?" I didn't know if I was happy or terrified.

"I'm pregnant, seven months from now a baby is set to come into this world and we don't even have a clear cut understanding as to what we are going to be to each other. You got this bitch that is ruining our family, and you can't seem to shake her no matter how wrong you know that it is." She sighed. "All I want is to be happy. I wanna be with my husband, my child, and my sister. That's not too much to ask." I was steering with my left hand while I looked over at her. "Ashlynn, are you serious?"

"Yeah, Tyson, I'm serious. I'm eight weeks. Your sister went to the gynecologist's office with me. She will confirm everything to you that I am saying." She sat back and crossed her arms in front of her. "So, now what are you going to do?"

"I don't give a fuck what goes on in life I am a man. Yo', if you really are about to have my Shorty then don't shit else matter but you. I don't give a fuck about how I feel about any other female because that shit will become nonexistent real fast." I pulled the car over to the curb, threw it in park, and pulled her shirt up. I kissed her stomach over and over again. "I'm sorry that I ever hurt you. I'm sorry that I ever lied to you." I kissed her stomach some more. "I'm sorry that I haven't taken the time to treat you like the Queen you deserve to be treated like. I owe you my life, Ashlynn. You are the mother and womb to my child." I laid my face sideways on her stomach, closing my eyes.

Then I was kissing all over it again. I even pulled the waistband of her jeans down some more so I could expose more of her belly. Then I was kissing and praying over it. Suddenly I became super overprotective of her.

She rested her hand on my head. "Thank you for saying those things. You have no idea how much hearing those words really mean to me. I have tried so hard to be the submissive wife to you. I have been one hundred percent faithful and devoted. I have bit my tongue more than you know and I have accepted things from you that I never thought that I would accept from any other man. Damn, Tyson, I am trying. I wasn't even going to tell you about this baby because I didn't think I would be strong enough to keep it, but then my conscious got the better of me. You are its father and you deserve to know about it coming into existence."

I kissed her belly some more before I sat up. I grabbed her face into my hands. "Listen to me, Ashlynn. I am sorry, and I promise to be better. I really care about you. Now that you are having our baby it is safe for me to say that I love you and I am ready to show you just how much. All I ask is that you work on forgiving me in your heart, please. Allow me to be the husband that I know I can be to you. Can you do that?" I looked into her eyes by using the dashboard lights and the streetlamps outside of the car. Rain pitter-pattered on the car loudly.

She was quiet for a long time. "Can we take it one day at a time. I need time to make sure that you really are going to change and that this isn't just you reacting to the news of becoming a father. Can you grant me time? That's all I ask."

"Yeah, ma, I can do that." I kissed her forehead and sat back. She did the same. I looked over at her. "Is this a murder mission?" I pulled the .45 from under my seat and placed it on my lap. According to the GPS we were only five minutes away from the address that she had given me.

"No, I have spoken to Odana. She is going to be ready and waiting for us. She will climb out of her bedroom window and we will go from there. Two bodyguards are doing occasional rounds to make sure that she is still put but other than that she is sure that her getaway will be a piece of cake. I hope we don't have to kill anybody but at the same time I love my sister and I am willing to do anything for her."

"And right hand to Jehovah I am willing to do whatever it takes on this mission as long as it gains your favor. I am with you one hundred percent."

She smiled. "Maybe I shoulda told you that I was pregnant sooner."

Ashlynn got out of the car that I had parked in the alley in Queens and stepped out into the rain. It was pouring down worse than ever. The thunder was loud and boisterous. Bright lightning flashed across the air every few seconds. The wind had picked up considerably. She stopped with her eyes squinted, her clothes became drenched right away and matted to her body. She waved to me to follow her. Then she took off running into the backyard of the house that Odana was supposed to be in.

I got out and followed her. We made it into the gangway just as a lightning bolt struck the power lines that were a hundred yards away from us. The entire block went dark for a few seconds and then the lights kicked back on.

Ashlynn counted the windows and stopped under the one I was guessing that Odana had told her she would be in. She stepped on her tippy toes and tapped on it. Her face was drenched with water. She waited for a few seconds and tapped again. About thirty seconds later the window raised but the first thing I noticed when I actually looked was that there were bars going parallel up and down the frame of the window. Odana stuck her face against them. She looked like a mirror image of Ashlynn, just younger and more exotic. Her eyes were an ice blue, and she was a shade darker.

Ashlynn made a squeaking sound. She stood up and laid her face against the bars. "Odana, where did these bars come from?"

"I don't know, they just put them on tonight before the rain. They are talking about putting locks on my room door. I have to get out of here. Please help me." She looked over her shoulder as if she were in a panic.

"How many men are in there with you? And what kind of guns are they handling?" I needed to know this so I could understand what I was getting myself into.

159

"It's two of them. They are small men with big guns. There is also a woman. She is nice to me. They are going off Garvey's orders. I still don't know why I am here?"

"I know why it's because of the damn war between the Deadly Guerillas and the Fast Money Cartel. But don't you worry I am going to get you out of here. By the way, this handsome man is Tyson. He is my husband."

Odana smiled through the bars. "It is nice to meet you, Tyson. Thank you for helping me."

"Come on, Tyson." Ashlynn pulled me by the wrist toward the front of the house.

When we got there and stepped onto the porch, she lowered her eyes and ripped her coat with one yank. Her supple breasts were wet and on display. She pressed the doorbell to the house and slipped her hand by her waistband pushing me to the side of the door. She placed her index finger to her lips.

The curtain moved a few times, and then it went back to normal seconds later the door opened and a tall, dark-skinned man stood in the doorway with an angry mug on his face. "Can I help you?"

"Uh, yes sir. I was just getting off my shift at the strip club when my car broke down. While trying to get to the nearest gas station I was robbed, and the man wound up getting away with my cell phone and my purse. Can I please use your phone?" She wiped some rainwater off her chest. Her titties looked real good, all wet and exposed the way they were. I ain't gon' lie she woulda even gotten me had I been in the dude's shoes.

"Yeah, Shorty that sounds cool. But if I let you use my phone what is you gon' give me?" He stepped out onto the porch a bit.

160

Ashlynn laughed, then quick as an assassin she had the same blade in her hand that she'd pulled on Tasia. She sliced it across the air three quick times. Blood spurt all over the porch and the man fell to the ground holding his neck. Ashlynn jumped over him and ran into the house.

I ran behind her after watching the man turn on to his back and reaching up for the sky while his blood formed a puddle around him on the porch. When we got into the house another man was sitting at the table tooting four lines of Heroin. He picked up his head. Ashlynn rushed him and slammed the knife into his Adam's apple. She pulled it out and slammed it into a different spot just left of his larynx. She took a step back and kicked him in the chest. He fell to the ground shaking.

A woman came out of the room screaming with her hands on her cheeks. Ashlynn threw the knife across the room with one flip of her wrist. It landed in the woman's chest. Ashlynn pulled a silenced .380 from her waist and popped the last three times. She hopped over her and kicked in Odana's room door. Odana ran out and into her arms. They hugged for what seemed like an eternity before I ordered us to get the hell out of there. My mind was blown from the way I'd watched Ashlynn get down. She had me kind of shook, I saw that she was more dangerous than I thought.

Chapter 19

It was a week after we recovered Odana from her captives, Maze hit my phone at 5:00 in the morning from the county jail saying that he needed me to come and pick him. He'd gotten pulled over coming back from Staten Island and the police had found a few stuffed blunts inside his ashtray, along with a bottle of Oxycontin. He was supposed to wait for a bail hearing but due to the fact that it was a nonviolent offense and the jails were overcrowded, they were letting him go with a hefty fine. I agreed to come and get him even though I was groggy as ever this morning.

Ashlynn and I had spent the whole night, previously, talking and getting to know each other on a higher level. Now that she was set to have my child, I wanted to really understand who she was as a woman. So, we talked and talked. Then when our mouths became so dry that we needed water to replenish them we talked some more. When we finally passed out it was 4:30 in the morning. So, at 5:30 when Maze called me, I wanted to punch somebody.

Ashlynn rolled over in the bed and grabbed the clock off the night table while I was up getting dressed. Odana was already up and watching the big screen without any sound. She had the caption going across the bottom of it.

Ashlynn looked at the clock with her face scrunched up. "What is going on? Why are you up so early making all of that noise?"

"I gotta go out for a minute. My nigga Maze gotta get picked up from the county jail. They're releasing him. I'll be right back. I just gotta go over to Staten Island."

"What?" Ashlynn sat up in bed and the covers fell off her exposing her naked breasts. "I'm supposed to believe that you are going to pick him up and not meet up with Tasia or somebody else. Yeah, the fuck right."

I frowned. "Yo', we just sat here for the last week having the best conversations ever. I thought we were getting a clear understanding. What, you still don't trust me or something?" I slipped my shirt over my head and grabbed my car keys.

I thought about grabbing my pistol too but the police were pulling everybody over and asking them where they were going, and when they would return home because the Governor of New York had put out a stay at home order for the entire state until the Coronavirus pandemic was over. I didn't want to get caught up in no bullshit, so I decided against grabbing my gun.

"Yeah, I trust you a'ight. I trust you so much that I am about to send Odana with you. She ain't doing shit anyway, besides that is your sister-in-law. Y'all need to get to know each other. Get up, Odana, and go with him."

Odana pulled the sheet off her and stood up in just her bra and panties. She began to get dressed. "How do we know that Garvey and the Deadly Guerillas aren't looking for me all over New York? What if they catch us out there and kill the both of us?"

"That's nonsense. King and I have already talked. You are going to be safe. I am pregnant, that's all King ever asked for. Besides, Garvey is too busy warring with King's army to worry about a prisoner. Y'all just need to go and come back," Ashlynn ordered.

"Aw man, why can't you just go. He's your husband." Odana shot the evil eye at her sister.

"Because you are going, and that's final. I got something I gotta do." Ashlynn stood up naked. She picked up her panties that were on the side of the bed and slipped them on. "Hurry up and go so y'all can get back. Oh, and while you're out,

Tyson, can you pick up a few items for me?" She grabbed her phone and texted me a list of things to grab from Walmart.

I read my phone and I wanted to curse her ass out. "Yo' I ain't fuckin' wit' Walmart, right now. The lines are wrapped around the block. Plus, early in the morning like this, they ain't letting nobody in but senior citizens."

"Well, I need every item on that list, so—" She walked up the stairs. "Make it happen." She disappeared upstairs.

I read over my phone. "Man, it's gon' take us all day to get this shit. Come on."

***

Odana turned down the Griselda track that I was bumping out of my speakers and looked over at me. She had to move her long reddish curly hair out of her face because she had the window slightly rolled down and it was blowing it everywhere. "I never did get a chance to tell you that I appreciate you for helping my sister get me out of that jam. You have no idea what those men were getting ready to do to me." She shook her head. "But seriously, though, thank you."

I looked over at her and smiled. "It's all good. I'm just glad that you are safe." I went back to looking at the road.

The scent of Odana's perfume was filling up the interiors of the car. I was trying my best to not pay attention to how fine she was. Though she and Ashlynn had a lot of similarities Odana was darker and had just a tad bit more weight on her. Her eyes were an ocean blue, and she seemed very quiet and laid back.

"So, what's the deal with you and my sister anyway? Are you two working things out?" She rested her arm on the window seal.

"We are a work in progress, but now that she is getting ready to have my child I gotta get my shit together. It's good, though."

"Yeah, well, I don't really know you like that, but you seem like a really good man. You two will figure it out. It takes time." She patted my right leg and squeezed it, then she went back to looking out of her window.

I would be lying if I said that what she'd just done didn't make me feel a way, but I pushed all those thoughts out of my mind quickly. Odana was my baby mother's sister. There was no way that I would ever think about crossing that line. I was better than that.

"Plus, you're fine too. I'll give Ashlynn that, she got a fine ass husband. Y'all will be a'ight."

I glanced over at her. "Yeah, we will be." Then I laughed with all kinds of crazy thoughts going through my mind that I'll keep to myself.

***

"Yo' Kid, it was mad disgusting up in there. They had mafuckas coming in there all kinds of sick. It's no wonder they were letting people off with a slap on the wrist. That Coronavirus shit is bad news. Who is Shorty right here? She's gorgeous!" Maze got into the back seat and closed the door.

"This my lil' sister, Odana. She's from Jamaica."

Maze held out his hand. "Nice to meet you, Little Miss Jamaica. How can I get to know you on a deeper level?"

She shook his hand and frowned at him. "I'm not interested but thank you for the compliment."

"Yo' ma, I don't know how yo' people get it in down there where you're from, but I'm from Brooklyn. I get mad chips.

You give me the time of day and I'ma change ya life. Word up." He kissed the back of her hand.

"Still not interested but thank you." She pulled her hand away from him and bucked her eyes at me. "I'm supposed to be ya like your sister and this is how you're protecting me, really?"

I laughed. "Maze is good people. He doesn't mean no harm." My phone buzzed, I picked it up and placed it to my ear. "What it do?"

"Tyson, please help me."

I eased my foot off the gas and pulled it to the side of the road. "Who dis?"

"It's Tasia, he's trying to kill me. He's in there beating the hell out of my mother. She's trying to stop him from getting to me. He swears that he wants me dead. Please help me."

"Who the fuck is doing this?" I snapped, hitting a U-turn heading toward Ms. Jazzy's house.

"Kammron he's fucked up off those drugs and alcohol. Please don't let him kill me," she whimpered.

"You're at your mother's house out in Brooklyn, right?" I asked, stepping on the gas a little more.

"Yeah, please hurry!" I could hear the beating on the door in the background, and then a loud bang. "Leave my mama alone, Daddy. Please leave her alone! Arrgh!" The phone went dead.

"Hello? Hello? Tasia? Tasia? Fuck!" I hung up and placed the phone on my lap.

"Yo' what the fuck was all of that about?" Maze asked, leaning over my seat.

"My sister told me to be on high alert for a bitch named Tasia. I take it, that was her?" Odana raised her right eyebrow.

"Tasia's daddy tripping. This nigga is trying to kill her and Ms. Jazzy. I get over there right away." I jumped on the highway.

"Fine ass Ms. Jazzy with all of the ass and body? Her nigga?" Maze shook his head and sighed loudly. "You betta have a pistol in dis mafucka if you talking about Kammron from Harlem. That nigga is crazy, and he stays wit' them hammers like he a Carpenter a somethin'."

"Yeah, I'm talking 'bout that nigga, but n'all I ain't got no pistol in here. I gotta stop at the crib real fast."

I sped all the way to Brooklyn and was surprised that I didn't get pulled over by the law. There were very few people out. When I pulled up to my parent's home I parked the car and rushed upon the stoop. My mother's car was gone. For a split second, I wondered where she could have gone but then remembered her being called into work that morning because she was a registered nurse and they were short on staff at the small hospital that she worked at because a lot of the nurses kept getting sick.

Hermés was sitting on the stoop with a black hood pulled over her head smoking a cigarette. She flicked it when I got to the top step. There were dark bags under her eyes. She stood up and held out her hands. "Tyson, I shoulda kept shit real with you in the beginning but I just didn't know how to."

I was in a frenzy. "Sis, I wanna holler at you but not right now. I gotta get in here and grab somethin' when I get back you and I need to talk okay?"

She held me for a second. "Just know that I wanted to tell you that it was never about you. I love you, go in there." She kissed my cheek.

I looked at her funny and then rushed into the house. I ran into the kitchen and directly to the back door. I pulled it open and hurried down the stairs knowing that time was of the essence when I hopped off the last step I almost had a heart attack from the sight before. There in the middle of the bed was Ashlynn. She was butt naked, moaning at the top of her lungs while my father King fucked her like a savage with her legs on top of his shoulders. When Ashlynn looked up and saw me, she tried to push King off her. His hips slammed into her back to back before he growled and shuddered while hugging her close to his body.

I laughed. "Yeah?"

King turned around and when he saw me his eyes got big. He slipped out of her and stood before me with his piece shining with her juices on it. "Son, I kin' explain."

I grabbed my gun and headed back toward the steps. "I ain't trippin'. Do what y'all do. All I wanna know is if that baby she is carrying is mine or yours?"

Ashlynn pulled the sheet around her body tighter and looked over at King. "Are you going to tell him what's really going on, or am I?"

To Be Continued...
King of the Trap 2
Coming Soon

Submission Guideline

Submit the first three chapters of your completed manuscript to ldpsubmissions@gmail.com, subject line: Your book's title. The manuscript must be in a .doc file and sent as an attachment. Document should be in Times New Roman, double spaced and in size 12 font. Also, provide your synopsis and full contact information. If sending multiple submissions, they must each be in a separate email.

Have a story but no way to send it electronically? You can still submit to LDP/Ca$h Presents. Send in the first three chapters, written or typed, of your completed manuscript to:

LDP: Submissions Dept
Po Box 944
Stockbridge, Ga 30281

DO NOT send original manuscript. Must be a duplicate.

Provide your synopsis and a cover letter containing your full contact information.

Thanks for considering LDP and Ca$h Presents.

Coming Soon from Lock Down Publications/Ca$h Presents

BOW DOWN TO MY GANGSTA

By **Ca$h**

TORN BETWEEN TWO

By **Coffee**

THE STREETS STAINED MY SOUL **II**

By **Marcellus Allen**

BLOOD OF A BOSS **VI**

SHADOWS OF THE GAME II

By **Askari**

LOYAL TO THE GAME **IV**

By **T.J. & Jelissa**

A DOPEBOY'S PRAYER **II**

By **Eddie "Wolf" Lee**

IF LOVING YOU IS WRONG… **III**

By **Jelissa**

TRUE SAVAGE **VII**

MIDNIGHT CARTEL III

DOPE BOY MAGIC IV

By **Chris Green**

BLAST FOR ME **III**

A SAVAGE DOPEBOY III

CUTTHROAT MAFIA II

By **Ghost**

A HUSTLER'S DECEIT III

KILL ZONE **II**

BAE BELONGS TO ME III

A DOPE BOY'S QUEEN II

By **Aryanna**

CHAINED TO THE STREETS III

By **J-Blunt**

COKE KINGS IV

KING OF THE TRAP II

By **T.J. Edwards**

GORILLAZ IN THE BAY V

TEARS OF A GANGSTA II

De'Kari

THE STREETS ARE CALLING II

Duquie Wilson

KINGPIN KILLAZ IV

STREET KINGS III

PAID IN BLOOD III

CARTEL KILLAZ IV

DOPE GODS II

Hood Rich

SINS OF A HUSTLA II

ASAD

TRIGGADALE III

Elijah R. Freeman

KINGZ OF THE GAME V

Playa Ray

SLAUGHTER GANG IV

RUTHLESS HEART IV

King of the Trap

By Destiny Skai

TOE TAGZ III

By Ah'Million

CONFESSIONS OF A GANGSTA II

By Nicholas Lock

I'M NOTHING WITHOUT HIS LOVE II

By Monet Dragun

CAUGHT UP IN THE LIFE II

By Robert Baptiste

NEW TO THE GAME III

By **Malik D. Rice**

LIFE OF A SAVAGE III

By **Romell Tukes**

QUIET MONEY II

By **Trai'Quan**

THE STREETS MADE ME II

By **Larry D. Wright**

THE ULTIMATE SACRIFICE VI

By **Anthony Fields**

THE LIFE OF A HOOD STAR

By Ca$h & Rashia Wilson

Available Now

RESTRAINING ORDER **I & II**

King of the Trap

By **CA$H & Coffee**
LOVE KNOWS NO BOUNDARIES **I II & III**
By **Coffee**
RAISED AS A GOON I, II, III & IV
BRED BY THE SLUMS I, II, III
BLAST FOR ME I & II
ROTTEN TO THE CORE I II III
A BRONX TALE I, II, III
DUFFEL BAG CARTEL I II III IV
HEARTLESS GOON I II III IV
A SAVAGE DOPEBOY I II
HEARTLESS GOON I II III
DRUG LORDS I II III
CUTTHROAT MAFIA
By **Ghost**
LAY IT DOWN **I & II**
LAST OF A DYING BREED
BLOOD STAINS OF A SHOTTA I & II III
By **Jamaica**
LOYAL TO THE GAME I II III
LIFE OF SIN I, II III
By **TJ & Jelissa**
BLOODY COMMAS I & II
SKI MASK CARTEL I II & III
KING OF NEW YORK I II,III IV V
RISE TO POWER I II III
COKE KINGS I II III

T.J. Edwards

BORN HEARTLESS I II III IV
KING OF THE TRAP
By **T.J. Edwards**
IF LOVING HIM IS WRONG…I & II
LOVE ME EVEN WHEN IT HURTS I II III
By **Jelissa**
WHEN THE STREETS CLAP BACK I & II III
THE HEART OF A SAVAGE I II
By **Jibril Williams**
A DISTINGUISHED THUG STOLE MY HEART I II & III
LOVE SHOULDN'T HURT I II III IV
RENEGADE BOYS I II III IV
PAID IN KARMA I II III
By **Meesha**
A GANGSTER'S CODE I &, II III
A GANGSTER'S SYN I II III
THE SAVAGE LIFE I II III
CHAINED TO THE STREETS I II
By J-Blunt
PUSH IT TO THE LIMIT
By **Bre' Hayes**
BLOOD OF A BOSS **I, II, III, IV, V**
SHADOWS OF THE GAME
By **Askari**
THE STREETS BLEED MURDER **I, II & III**
THE HEART OF A GANGSTA I II& III
By **Jerry Jackson**

176

CUM FOR ME I II III IV V

An **LDP Erotica Collaboration**

BRIDE OF A HUSTLA **I II & II**

THE FETTI GIRLS **I, II& III**

CORRUPTED BY A GANGSTA I, II III, IV

BLINDED BY HIS LOVE

THE PRICE YOU PAY FOR LOVE

DOPE GIRL MAGIC

By **Destiny Skai**

WHEN A GOOD GIRL GOES BAD

By **Adrienne**

THE COST OF LOYALTY I II III

By Kweli

A GANGSTER'S REVENGE **I II III & IV**

THE BOSS MAN'S DAUGHTERS I II III IV V

A SAVAGE LOVE **I & II**

BAE BELONGS TO ME I II

A HUSTLER'S DECEIT I, II, III

WHAT BAD BITCHES DO I, II, III

SOUL OF A MONSTER I II III

KILL ZONE

A DOPE BOY'S QUEEN

By **Aryanna**

A KINGPIN'S AMBITON

A KINGPIN'S AMBITION **II**

I MURDER FOR THE DOUGH

By **Ambitious**

T.J. Edwards

TRUE SAVAGE I II III IV V VI
DOPE BOY MAGIC I, II, III
MIDNIGHT CARTEL I II
By **Chris Green**
A DOPEBOY'S PRAYER
By **Eddie "Wolf" Lee**
THE KING CARTEL **I, II & III**
By **Frank Gresham**
THESE NIGGAS AIN'T LOYAL **I, II & III**
By **Nikki Tee**
GANGSTA SHYT **I II &III**
By **CATO**
THE ULTIMATE BETRAYAL
By **Phoenix**
BOSS'N UP **I , II & III**
By **Royal Nicole**
I LOVE YOU TO DEATH
By Destiny J
I RIDE FOR MY HITTA
I STILL RIDE FOR MY HITTA
By **Misty Holt**
LOVE & CHASIN' PAPER
By **Qay Crockett**
TO DIE IN VAIN
SINS OF A HUSTLA
By **ASAD**
BROOKLYN HUSTLAZ

King of the Trap

By **Boogsy Morina**
BROOKLYN ON LOCK I & II
By **Sonovia**
GANGSTA CITY
By **Teddy Duke**
A DRUG KING AND HIS DIAMOND I & II III
A DOPEMAN'S RICHES
HER MAN, MINE'S TOO I, II
CASH MONEY HO'S
By Nicole Goosby
TRAPHOUSE KING **I II & III**
KINGPIN KILLAZ I II III
STREET KINGS I II
PAID IN BLOOD **I II**
CARTEL KILLAZ I II III
DOPE GODS
By **Hood Rich**
LIPSTICK KILLAH **I, II, III**
CRIME OF PASSION I II & III
By **Mimi**
STEADY MOBBN' **I, II, III**
THE STREETS STAINED MY SOUL
By **Marcellus Allen**
WHO SHOT YA **I, II, III**
SON OF A DOPE FIEND
Renta
GORILLAZ IN THE BAY **I II III IV**

T.J. Edwards

TEARS OF A GANGSTA
DE'KARI
TRIGGADALE I II
Elijah R. Freeman
GOD BLESS THE TRAPPERS I, II, III
THESE SCANDALOUS STREETS I, II, III
FEAR MY GANGSTA I, II, III
THESE STREETS DON'T LOVE NOBODY I, II
BURY ME A G I, II, III, IV, V
A GANGSTA'S EMPIRE I, II, III, IV
THE DOPEMAN'S BODYGAURD
Tranay Adams
THE STREETS ARE CALLING
Duquie Wilson
MARRIED TO A BOSS… I II III
By Destiny Skai & Chris Green
KINGZ OF THE GAME I II III IV
Playa Ray
SLAUGHTER GANG I II III
RUTHLESS HEART I II III
By Willie Slaughter
FUK SHYT
By Blakk Diamond
DON'T F#CK WITH MY HEART I II
By Linnea
ADDICTED TO THE DRAMA I II III
By Jamila

King of the Trap

YAYO I II

A SHOOTER'S AMBITION I II

By S. Allen

TRAP GOD

By Troublesome

FOREVER GANGSTA

GLOCKS ON SATIN SHEETS

By Adrian Dulan

TOE TAGZ I II

By Ah'Million

KINGPIN DREAMS

By Paper Boi Rari

CONFESSIONS OF A GANGSTA

By Nicholas Lock

I'M NOTHING WITHOUT HIS LOVE

By Monet Dragun

CAUGHT UP IN THE LIFE

By Robert Baptiste

NEW TO THE GAME I II

By **Malik D. Rice**

Life of a Savage I II

By **Romell Tukes**

LOYALTY AIN'T PROMISED

By Keith Williams

Quiet Money

By **Trai'Quan**

THE STREETS MADE ME

T.J. Edwards

By **Larry D. Wright**
THE ULTIMATE SACRIFICE I, II, III, IV, V
KHADIFI
By **Anthony Fields**
THE LIFE OF A HOOD STAR
By **Ca$h & Rashia Wilson**

BOOKS BY LDP'S CEO, CA$H

TRUST IN NO MAN
TRUST IN NO MAN 2
TRUST IN NO MAN 3
BONDED BY BLOOD
SHORTY GOT A THUG
THUGS CRY
THUGS CRY 2
THUGS CRY 3
TRUST NO BITCH
TRUST NO BITCH 2
TRUST NO BITCH 3
TIL MY CASKET DROPS
RESTRAINING ORDER
RESTRAINING ORDER 2
IN LOVE WITH A CONVICT
LIFE OF A HOOD STAR

Coming Soon
BONDED BY BLOOD 2
BOW DOWN TO MY GANGSTA